"Cicellis . . . looks at life steadily and as if for the first time, with profound watchfulness, as if nothing else mattered. That is her essential originality; she has her own vision of life . . . She is fascinated by certain kinds of experience, especially those in which the imagination seems to grow transparent, so that all things are reflected in it, and everything is in its place . . . Cicellis takes life from many sides, and is always sensitively conscious of the quality of the situation she describes. She has a style which catches the intimate nature of things and never stops at the surface. She is a remarkable writer."

—Edwin Muir, *The Observer*

"Cicellis . . . has a startling talent, and her fluent precision lends a kind of dignity to the characters she creates."

—Marigold Johnson, *Times Literary Supplement*

"She is like Penelope at her web, shuttling the coloured threads to and fro, weaving into the pattern love and hate, laughter and death . . . infinitely subtle."

—Peter Green, *Daily Telegraph*

"War and circumstance have made her an English writer of high intelligence and great perspicaciousness exactly expressed."

—Martin Shuttleworth, *The Listener*

"The characters in these Greek stories burn in that enclosed air of people living, damned, within the rigid context of their emotions. Existence is an imposition which all recognise and none avoids."

—David Storey, *Sunday Times*

THE WAY TO COLONOS

THE WAY TO COLONOS

SOPHOCLES RETOLD

KAY CICELLIS

WITH A FOREWORD BY RACHEL CUSK

McNally Editions

New York

McNally Editions
134 Prince St.
New York, NY 10012

Printed in the United States of America
Originally published in 1960 by Secker and Warburg, London
First McNally Editions paperback, 2025

ISBN: 978-1-94602-277-6
E-book: 978-1-94602-278-3

Design by Jonathan Lippincott

1 3 5 7 9 10 8 6 4 2

CONTENTS

FOREWORD

This savage little book is a recasting of three Sophoclean tragedies into the modern era. It unfolds for its reader certain human situations that are familiar enough, with an absence of sentimentality that renders them entirely shocking and strange. Its themes are the pain of youth and the disillusionment that comes with observing the less than faithful relationship between authority figures and the truth, but its originality resides in its broaching of the force of tragedy in ordinary human relationships. This is not to say that existence is presented as merely nihilistic or absurd: on the contrary, the characters here are beset by almost ungovernable emotion. What is tragic is the infallibility with which their natural love of justice and truth is taken from the hands of these young protagonists and bruised or broken by the people on whom they rely—rely not just for survival but for the explanation of life and the example of how to live it that their elders are meant to provide.

Born to Greek parents in Marseille in 1926, Kay Cicellis was educated in English and only began to learn

Greek at the age of thirteen on the family's return to Athens. English remained her language for writing, and at the age of twenty-two she produced a collection of stories that appears to have been widely reviewed in the anglophone world. *The Easy Way* is a fascinating document as well as a text of great literary merit. It is almost impossible to credit it as the work of a very young woman writing in a language not her own. It isn't only, as Vita Sackville-West observed in her introduction to the first edition, that despite never having even been to England "she writes English as though she were English born . . . in all [her] stories I have never detected one single phrase which in its syntax or its parenthetical composition could not have come from a born-English pen." The stories have the muscularity and dark-bloodedness of D. H. Lawrence's short fiction, their absence of unconscious constraint by social class and conditioning. Lawrence gave voice to a new sound in fiction: his sentences felt different in the ear, because he didn't come from somewhere his readers recognised. Kay Cicellis likewise was unidentifiable by any of the means through which writers generally betray themselves. The stories in *The Easy Way* are set in—mostly rural—Greece, but there is no knowing how or why their narrator is there. The cool, clear, granite-like objectivity of this young writer's voice is like a flooding of daylight into the stuffy chambers of descriptive prose. Reading it, two questions arise: Is it the case that literature's besetting weaknesses generally arise from the involuntary subjectivity of a cultural identity? And might it be true—because Kay Cicellis did not attain with her subsequent novels the success and renown this startling beginning seemed to promise—that a writer's fate is nonetheless bound to the life that comes to her, to the time and place in which she finds herself and by which—talent notwithstanding—her oeuvre stands or falls? Kay Cicellis created in the very midst of this contradiction, an outstanding writer with the wrong material in her hands. Midcentury Greece, peripheral, poor and backward-looking, was an inadequate canvas for the expansion of her gifts. Unlike Natalia Ginzburg's, her life did not seem to offer her the intersection of the personal with the political that could provide a foothold for her voice.

The Way to Colonos is a magnificent resolution of this problem, written in an ageless prose that instantly strikes the reader as the work of a master. The Greece that is its setting is here abstracted into simple forms—island, city, suburb, boat—while its human characters are enlarged into all their involuntary violence and torment. These three tales use myth as a means not of aggrandising but of clarifying and sharpening situations that otherwise would be muddied and burdened by explanation. Cicellis's Antigone is a young woman hardened by disgust at her parents' dreadful marriage who finds more truth in lying and in sex than in her father's pathetic and hypocritical morality. Electra is also paralysed by disgust at the conduct of adults and their limitless capacity for self-justification, yet in her case it is her starved and suffocated love for her mother—her need to love her, unworthy as she is—that torments her. In the final story, Sophocles's less-known play *Philoctetes* is transformed into another instance of youthful disappointment when a young man trying to assume the mantle of masculinity is deeply disillusioned by the conduct of older men he viewed as heroes. Their sculpted brevity—each could easily have been a novel—makes newly shocking the recognisability of these situations; indeed, reading them, the usual long arc of contemporary prose narrative comes to seem more and more like a morally questionable scheme of habituation, a process by which readers acquire tolerance for what ought to arouse the strongest passions and responses.

This book, written when Cicellis was in her midthirties, is especially striking for what it shares with her earliest work: a wholly convincing belief in the power and moral authority of youth. In her first stories it was the precocious Cicellis herself who demonstrated this power; in *The Way to Colonos* she retains a burning understanding of a period of life fraught with growth and blight, in which the burgeoning human spirit is met by continuous attempts to deform and constrain it. The earlier work sought to trace the social and environmental factors driving this loss of innocence; these later stories, with their deep foundation of myth, can ascribe more significance to fate. It is as though, with hindsight, Cicellis can suddenly see how much of the dynamic agony and joy of being young comes from the unknowability of the future. Faced with the great blank of what is to come, what is appears infinitely negotiable and escapable. It is this—this elemental trust in the concept of freedom and free will—that constitutes the force of tragedy in human development. With a subtle intelligence, what Cicellis grasps in these stories is that her young protagonists claim as a freedom the right to hate or disapprove of the adults who hold so-called authority over them, when the forces of tragedy and fate have already decreed that no such freedom exists. Their struggle with these figures, which they mistake for a threshold into a realm of election, is in fact a struggle against predestiny itself, for what the mothers and fathers in all their disappointing reality represent is the inalienable fixity of the world we are born into and of mortality itself.

The contradiction of myth lies in its eternal submersion of knowledge in the face of experience: it is the proof from which we never learn, the touchstone we only recognise afterwards, when we have already lost our way. By applying this tragic formulation to the ordinariness of the parent-child relationship, Cicellis extracts something of greater boldness and truth from the fictional situation. There can, in other words, be no happy resolution, such as fiction is always tempted to offer; the question of how parents and parent-figures gain and retain their power, and what becomes of the child's illusion of freedom, is already foretold. In "The Return," the figures of Electra and Clytemnestra are a mother and daughter locked in a vicious dependency: their mutual loathing is not a springboard to separation but the cyclical expression of a need for love of a kind neither can offer the other. Cicellis's Antigone, in the title story, has become a jaded liar as the consequence of parental control: "having lived under oppression all her life, deception was in the nature of things. . . . The contractions of appearances had ceased to puzzle her. Misunderstanding had become a definite, but unimportant, necessity; she had found it need no longer exclude reality."

Both stories offer shocking insight into the secret lives of young women as they writhe beneath parental scrutiny, learning instinctively how to deceive and dissimulate while remaining heartbreakingly in need of nurture and love. Despite their grounding in myth, these are recognisably modern situations in which the powerful carapace of family unity has already cracked—the parental unit, that twosome that blocks the exit and lays down the lifelong foundations for existence being experienced as a form of narrative, has been sundered. These young people have already been stripped of a different kind of myth, the myth of meaning and order that the family structure imposes on new minds. Through the cracks they see the hypocrisy and selfishness and self-justifying weakness of the adults among whom nonetheless they remain trapped. In "The Exile" the same disillusionment arises, this time in the matrix of military life, when a young recruit is brought to question the courage and honour he naturally ascribes to his superiors. The myth on which it is based is *Philoctetes*, "one of the few ancient plays," as Cicellis writes in her foreword, "in which there is no hero." In the play, Philoctetes is a key player in the Trojan war who has been abandoned by his army on a deserted island after a snake bite to his foot renders him disabled. Ten years later the army—in the person of Odysseus and the young Neoptolemus—is forced to come and find him after it has become clear that the war cannot be won without him. Philoctetes is the possessor of Heracles's bow, the vital weapon for victory, and the innocent Neoptolemus comes to realise that Odysseus intends not to rescue Philoctetes but merely to steal the bow and leave him in his agonising exile.

It is perhaps Sophocles's most intriguing work, for its themes of suffering and injustice are so specifically and tangibly human and its characters so ambivalent and lifelike. Pain and unfairness have made Philoctetes depressed and incapable of forgiveness; ambition has made Odysseus immoral. Between them, the child Neoptolemus ponders the nature of justice and right, where the communal need to win the war is weighed against the personal betrayal and theft of Philoctetes. With the idealism of his youth, Cicellis's Neoptolemus instinctively sides with—and attempts to idolise—the injured man, only to discover what suffering and injustice do to the human spirit. Philoctetes here is broken and deadened by loneliness and pain—he can no longer love or hope. "You offered me a role," he later tells the young man. "I took it . . . I jumped at it. It didn't last long. But nothing so good had come my way for a long time. You gave me something to do. You gave me something to be. What did you expect?" At this bald admission from an adult, the young man "shuddered a little, half pride, half horror. He had given birth, unknowingly; it was the first time; and the child was a monster."

Today's reader of Kay Cicellis will find in her voice another missing piece of the female literary puzzle, a woman before her time in her scrutiny of intimate relationships and her effortless shrugging off of the conventions that adhere both to the living and to the representation of them. She is a writer who has lacked a category, and it is to be hoped that her writing will now find itself beyond categorisation, free to reach readers with an appetite for female artistic authority who wish to see the world through sharp, fresh eyes.

Rachel Cusk
Paris, 2024

AUTHOR'S NOTE

In an early book called *Feux*, Marguerite Yourcenar says: "ce qui compte dans la légende et le mythe est leur capacité de nous servir de pierre de touche, d'alibi . . ." Perhaps that is the only valid justification for a modern writer who attempts to rehandle ancient myths. It is a process that does need some kind of justification. There is always a vague feeling of plagiarism, even of desecration, especially if—as in my case—the myths have already been used by one of the great ancient playwrights. But worse than these is the sense of pointlessness. It is so easy to slip into pointlessness when using this kind of material; pointlessness either because you stick too close to the myth and are merely putting it into different words—and then why do it, since it has been done before, only better. Or you refashion it completely until the myth is almost unrecognizable, and then again why do it, since obviously the story can stand on its own feet and does not need the crutches of the myth. It is very hard to keep a balance between the two; to retain the echoes, which add depth, and to bring a new note, that will alter the sound without disfiguring it.

I started the first of these three stories, quite simply, as an exercise in objectiveness. I suppose I wanted an alibi too; I wanted the sharp fresh contact of a subject—or a character—completely alien to myself. I soon found out nothing is completely alien to oneself, or rather one does not allow it to remain alien; the personal creeps in. But meanwhile in this new territory I also found out other things, more fascinating; all the problems of translation. Translating the myth into a modern setting was the most obvious; putting the characters not only into modern dress, but into modern flesh. But more interesting was the translation from theatre to prose. I don't mean this only in the technical sense; the translation into prose affected the very essence of the story; the psychology, the situations, the atmosphere. In the end of course this problem became linked to the problem of time-translation, since the play, as a literary form, could be called timeless, whereas prose is much more of our time. The idea was to bring the story out of the long ago, the fixed, clear, pure remote archetype down into the tangle of prose, of a prose-world. Very often it is the other way round; one starts from the tangle, from the actual particular case and threads one's way back to the hidden archetype, the universal. This time it was away from an archetype already known instead of back to it, a deliberate narrowing down to the particular. So there had to be a breaking-down of the fixed patterns, a dilution of the concentrated meanings, till they became more fluid and could circulate more easily into the stream of a modern consciousness, through the ramified channels of prose as we now know it. The action became more indirect; the motives less clear-cut;

the behaviour ambiguous; the picture re-drawn but with shadows put in, like another dimension; the crimes, the initial crimes that usually lie at the root of all these myths, became crimes of omission rather than crimes of hubris; and the notion of heroism almost completely disappeared.

Yet however far from the archetype the story drifted, the myth never lost its power. I always felt it at my back, giving me a peculiar assurance, a sense of reality and a sense of direction. If it was a bondage, it was never oppressive—the road was both traced and unknown. Rather than a bondage, it was more a subterranean body of associations, such as there always are, no matter what one writes, only in this case a more organic one.

All three stories are based on plays by Sophocles; but this is only a coincidence. In each of the stories, the link with the original myth is different; the link is dictated by the story itself. There is no formula, I don't think there can be; that is why I didn't stop at the first one; each story was a new problem, and the fascination persisted.

The Way to Colonos is based on *Oedipus at Colonos*, but the character of Antigone also includes some of the aspects of her character as shown in the "Antigone." In this story, it is Antigone herself, the quality, the flavour, the inner shape of Antigone that provides the link—even though she is no longer pure, innocent and virtuous; but for me the important thing about Antigone is not her virtue or innocence but her almost ruthless sense of justice and truth—she is not primarily a creature of love. That is why she is the only character in the story who keeps her name; she bears it like a title, it is part of her.

In "The Return," the link with the myth is the initial situation; it is more or less the same as in the play. Only there I followed a kind of hunch, an instinctive, obsessive feeling that has always made me believe that Orestes was reluctant to exercise vengeance, not really interested; and that Electra was much closer to her mother than she thought. And so the story developed along these lines, perhaps more naturally, as well as more sordidly, than in the play, since the story was now free of the two ancient imperatives, duty and fatality; and finally reaches a conclusion entirely different from the one in the play. Here the only character to retain his ancient name is Orestes, not for the same reason as Antigone, but because he is an instrument, he is functional and he must be known by his exact appellation.

"The Exile" was to me the most interesting of the three stories; because there are far more conflicts in it, and because from the start Philoctetes is not a hero; it is one of the few ancient plays in which there is no hero. So the process of "prosification" was more complicated. Here not only the situation is the same, but the conclusion as well; it is the motives that have changed. I have kept none of the ancient names in this one, because all the characters have been refashioned—being lesser known, lesser fixed than Antigone, Electra, Orestes, they are more fluid, more subject to varied interpretation.

THE WAY TO COLONOS

An old man in a wheelchair, a young girl dressed in black: these two were the first to board the ship. The other first-class passengers, who climbed on deck just before the ship sailed, came upon them suddenly; an odd couple, sitting quite motionless near the railings. They must have been there for hours. They were looking out to sea—the docks, the rusty cargoes, the white liners—as if they were already travelling.

Their stillness was broken only when the girl rose and offered her deck-chair to a woman among the passengers: there were no other chairs and the woman was elderly. This gesture of politeness was executed coldly, like a mere act of justice. The girl did not even look at the woman; her eyes were kept lowered throughout her impersonal operation. The woman accepted the chair uneasily.

There were not many passengers in the first class. A few merchants, a few landowners and rich farmers; no tourists. They were mostly people going back somewhere, back home, back to some unchanging point of departure, after an interlude in the capital. This was not a pleasure trip. All the pleasure, if any, lay behind, in the receding harbour. The third class was slightly more crowded, because there were animals: a great many hens, bunched together like vegetables, and a dozen skinny cows. After only half an hour, the cows had soiled the lower deck so badly that people threading their way aft to the third-class lavatory lost their balance on the slippery boards.

The ship was not punctual in sailing. The captain did not care. The passengers were unimportant. His ship was on the "Barren Line," which means that it was subsidized by the State to serve outlying islands, itineraries which could not possibly yield any profit. Once a fortnight—once a week in summer—the ship started on its long, slow, winding journey, stopping in many small ports, where the warmth of the islanders' welcome, the excitement caused by the ship's arrival—contrasting with the indifference of the busier islands—did not quite succeed in mellowing the captain's sour disposition. Like most of the "Barren Line" captains, he felt frustrated. He missed the hustle and bustle of the worldlier ships, the quarrels, the incidents, the bribes for non-existent cabin space, the singing and drinking in the third class, the dancing to the gramophone in the first class. He also missed the tourists, the foreigners. For this reason he had been especially nice to the old man and the girl in black; (it was he who had brought out the deck-chair for the girl) for though they spoke Greek, they looked like strangers; their faces were unfamiliar, and there was a vague shabby distinction about them.

He was curious about them; he thought of getting their names from the chief steward. But it would have to wait.

Now he was busy steering the ship out of the harbour. The winter afternoon was coming to an end, hurriedly. The dirty sea took on a brief, steely glint which was all the sunset could give it. Then the electric lights took over in the houses, shops and ships, all at once and so masterfully that one wasn't sure they hadn't been on all through the grey afternoon.

The harbour boomed and echoed for a while around the passengers on deck; then suddenly there was only the clapping of the waves against the flanks of the ship. They were out at sea, on their own. Some of the passengers, already bored, went down to the smoking-room. The old man and the girl remained; they were still motionless, their backs turned to the other people. The girl now stood beside the wheelchair, her hand on the old man's shoulder.

One of the few remaining passengers on deck, a currant-merchant, turned to his friend: "What about dinner?"

"We might as well wait till after the Corinth Canal," the friend said with a sigh.

"Of course. . . ."

It took the ship about half an hour to crawl through the narrow canal. The rest of the passengers came back on deck for it. They had also thought: "One might as well wait till after the Canal." But there was no real excitement. There were no tourists to click their cameras. Most of the people on board had been through the Canal a dozen times. But they had waited for it in order to pass the time; to postpone an early, unwanted dinner, to postpone going to bed in the stuffy cabins; and to split up time in smaller, more manageable doses.

"Why don't you come and stand here, you will get a better view of it," said the currant-merchant to the girl in black, stepping away from the railings. The girl shook her head, and turned her face in the other direction. She seemed to be very shy, not to say prim.

Down in the dining-room, the old man remembered the incident with an effort: "What did that man say to you," he asked the girl, "while we were going through the Canal?"

"He wanted me to take his place, so as to see better."

"So that was what he said. I can't hear well, I can't see well. But you know what to do in such cases, you know how to look after yourself. Thank God, yes, you know what to do."

She accepted his praise demurely. He picked up his fork and began to eat, quite greedily. But the girl stopped him, her hand on his sleeve. "Father, your medicine."

He stopped eating, he closed his eyes. "No, no," he sighed, "why should I?"

"It is here," the girl said dubiously. But she was very calm.

"Why should I, why should I?" he repeated in despair. "Why should I be kept fit? Why should I be kept alive?"

She looked at him steadily, her fingers curled round the cap of the small medicine bottle. She insisted a little with her eyes, then no more. Once again, she had performed an act of justice, a duty, that was all. Otherwise, one might have said she agreed with him; or rather she did not particularly want to encourage a different attitude in him.

"Was I talking too loud?" he asked anxiously, after a pause.

"No, it is all right. We are alone. You can talk as if you were alone."

They ate on in silence.

The captain sat two tables away from them. The girl was right, he could not hear what they were saying. But he had noticed the tiny muffled scene over the medicine. He had not thought much about it; however it did remind him that he would like to get their names from the chief steward. He sent for him.

The captain was alone at his table. On the first few trips he had tried to organize "the captain's table," as he had heard the captains on big liners did. But it hadn't worked. The passengers on this line didn't understand that sort of thing. They thought it meant that he was offering them a free meal, inviting them. Also, they were very dull people, for the most part. The captain was not interested in the currant market. So tonight, as usual, he ate alone. He felt he could watch the couple better if he knew their names. Perhaps it would be a well-known name? An old, distinguished family from the islands . . .

The waiter came back, and whispered the name in the captain's ear. "And she's his daughter," he added. "They come from Zante, but they haven't been there for years. The steward said the old gentleman's wife died a month ago."

The captain had not heard of their name before. He was disappointed, a bit. Now he noticed their shabbiness without their distinction, and also the fact that they were having a very frugal meal. They had ordered only one course, and not even a meat or fish course: a greasy pilaf, and then some fruit.

The waiter stooped again: "One of our cabin-boys is from Zante. Perhaps he has heard of them."

The girl was beautiful, in a stale sort of way. She was pale and her skin was not very good, except for the forehead, which was extraordinarily pure. She wore no makeup; her hair hung on her shoulders, quite long. Her figure, too, was rather bad; and her black dress, old-fashioned, did not help it; it was closed at the neck and the sleeves were long, like a schoolgirl's pinafore. But she had a wonderful profile; cold, too Grecian to be seductive, but wonderful all the same; and fine brown eyes with clashing brows, and small even teeth. It was not the kind of beauty that would ever "blossom" forth; it would always be a little cramped, a little faded; and it would harden with the years.

Her father was more ordinary. He had a slight paunch, and he was going bald. He wore black-rimmed glasses. His mouth, rather thick-lipped, sagged, a sign of disgust and indulgence at the same time. His black tie was very thick and badly knotted. But she kept him scrupulously clean; that was obvious. He was by no means "venerable"; the only trace of nobility was in his pallor—his invalid's pallor; and in his thin, tremulous hands, freckled with age.

He gave Antigone his hands to be helped back into his wheelchair. He could hobble about on crutches when necessary, but he spent most of his time in the wheelchair.

•

"Antigone, Antigone, I am already so tired; and it is only the first day. Were we right to go away? Was I right to accept your suggestion? But there was not much else we could do. I agree with you there. After your mother died, the rent-control people would soon have made us leave the house. It was much too big for two people, they kept saying. One wouldn't have thought that one person less could have made all that difference . . . Besides, it would have been too expensive; we couldn't afford to stay. My poor child, it is time I told you these things; because you must take over now. It galls me to have to tell you this. But you must take over. And you are so young! I should be able to support you, take care of you. But I can't. I am old; look at me, don't turn away your face: I am a useless invalid. Of course, I can still take care of you in some ways; I hope so; but not materially. For the past ten years, we have been living on the salary your mother got as a teacher; on that alone. You knew that? How could you not know, she repeated it often enough. You must never say anything against your mother, Antigone; she was a fine woman, in spite of her faults. Believe me, she was heroic. A prosaic, unglamorous hero, which makes her even finer; a domestic hero. Alas, heroes often tend to become tyrants. That is how it is. I am not complaining. I never complained—you must understand this. I must never see in your eyes the dreadful suspicion I kept meeting in the faces of her relatives during the whole month that followed her death. I would not be able to bear that; I would not forgive it, as your father. I am still your father, in spite of what has happened. I am still your father. You are very young, and you need me. I think that is the only thing that keeps me alive. I am now a man with no rights; I am entitled to nothing; but at least I have a few duties left. Sometimes I forget, I give up, I think I ought to die. I will try not to be weak. I promise you I will try not to repeat that scene over my medicine. One tries to punish oneself, as best one can. Those hideous relatives of hers, they have undermined my spirit. You never liked her relatives much either, did you? From the first day of our marriage, they kept saying that nothing good could come of a marriage between first cousins. I can still prove them wrong; that is one of my duties. Through you, Antigone. You will prove them wrong. My Antigone. You are a beautiful child. But I must not tell you this too often. Don't ask why. Did you know that when you were small, I never noticed you much? I had too many worries, I suppose. Until the day of the accident, I had never paid real attention to you. Then, on that terrible morning, you stepped out of the shadows, as it were. . . . You were there; and you have never ceased being there since that day. You led me to this ship. You have almost become a part of me; I say almost, because my guilt separates us. I have often thought: Do I deserve you, after what I have done? I know there are many people who believe I do not deserve a daughter like you—so devoted, so obedient. Perhaps they are right. No, you must not try to comfort me. I am a miserable man. I must face what I have done. There is some truth in what her relatives say. I was not much good to your mother. From the day we married everything seemed to go wrong. As a breadwinner I was a terrible failure. Bad luck dogged everything I did. Then I got my first stroke. . . . It made me very bitter—do you blame me? It should have killed me then and there; or at least the second stroke should have, on the morning of the accident. It would have been more merciful. But who am I to ask for mercy? I keep forgetting what I have done. I must not forget. You must remind me. I mean that; it is an order. I am still your father, after all. And yet, and yet—why didn't she ring that doorbell a little longer? I would have heard her in the end, I would have opened the door. I did not mean to lock her out all night. Why did she have to walk off in the rain like that? One would have thought she *wanted* to get killed. Perhaps she did. Perhaps I made her want to get killed. You see? You see? You won't dare say anything in my defence now. Antigone, what I did was terrible, never forget that."

As they went up on deck, she had said to him once again: "No one can hear us. You can speak as if we were alone; as if you were alone." (She did not count. She was just there.) So now there was this long monologue against the sea-wind, which sounded exactly like their silences. The passengers could not hear, but they watched and they whispered among themselves their incomplete information, snatched from captain and steward. "A widower—she died a month ago (a tragic death)—he looks so broken—no wonder—poor man (and she) so young—life is a sad business (life is)—poor man—girl—" The whispers died away on the wind. There was not much to say, really. Simple sorrow leads to a dead end, like perfect joy. The sorrow of death is the simplest of all. Simple sorrow is not sufficient. Antigone knew that well.

She waited to see whether his monologue would fluctuate once more between self-accusation and self-justification, shame and rebellion, the old pendulum swinging back and forth. But he was quiet now, waiting. So she gave him his echo; she said: “Yes, I suppose it was a terrible thing. What you did was a terrible thing.” He looked at her gratefully, wounded, his eyes swimming, letting her cool words sting him in a pure, delicious silence of acceptance.

Meanwhile Antigone thought: “It was not really terrible. I have lied to him again, as I used to do in the days before the accident. It must be my fate, always to lie to him.”

The first big lie had been a year ago, when she was eighteen and she decided to spend a whole night out with her lover. She had had to find a good excuse, plan things carefully. It had not been easy. Her father was very old- fashioned; he posed as a patriarchal parent, he believed in bringing her up strictly. He forbade her to wear makeup, to smoke, to go dancing. One day he had found her putting curlers in her hair, and had slapped her face, outraged. Her mother was not so vigilant; she was out most of the day, and in the evenings, exhausted by several strenuous hours of teaching, she didn’t care. Antigone tried to keep clear of her father. She succeeded, because except on matters of discipline, he did not seem much aware of her existence. He spent all his hours in his wheelchair, brooding, reading the morning paper, reading old letters from business associates who had abandoned him long ago, looking over the household accounts. As he could have no part in the earning of the household money, he soothed his vanity by taking over the responsibility for the accounts; he did them meticulously. Money had always been the sore point between Antigone’s parents. All their quarrels were caused by money. The proud man even depended on his wife for pocket-money. He had to ask her for it, nicely; he had to realise, with a fresh shock every time, that all his account-holding was but a shadow, and the reality lay in his wife's hand, in her worn black handbag.

For her mother Antigone had a kind of understanding, of tacit approval and ease, which was almost love. For her father she had nothing. For this reason she had no pangs in telling him lies, in deceiving him. She did it with beautiful cold-bloodedness. Hers was not an affectionate nature, anyway. But though she had no pangs, she was often puzzled, torn, made uneasy by the blatant contradiction between reality and appearance. She could not understand how they could exist side by side: her secret life, her secret thoughts, her real self, and the life she appeared to lead, the person her father believed her to be. It seemed to her amazing—wrong even—that the two aspects should not influence each other: that reality did not betray the nullity of appearance, that the falsity of appearance did not corrode reality. Sometimes she simply thought she was mad. Then once again she would get used to seeing things double. She would obediently pay her due to appearance; she would tell lies; she would resume her place in the void that existed between her father and herself.

For the purpose of spending the night with her lover, she had made up quite a complicated story. A friend of hers—a girl from school—had had an operation, appendicitis to be precise. After a week in hospital, the girl was to come back to her house. She wanted Antigone to keep her company during this first night of convalescence; she might need something, she might have a relapse. Normally the girl lived with her aunt; but her aunt, it seemed, was away in Salonica and would not be back till two days later. Antigone must go; she could not let her friend down.

But would Antigone—young, inexperienced—be able to look after a girl who had recently been operated on, in an emergency? Antigone hardly seemed the right person for a case like this, her father objected.

Antigone said that another person—an older woman—had half-promised to come as well; but it was not certain. She must be there in case the other woman did not come. There was a doctor living next door; she would go to him in an emergency.

Her parents asked her what was the girl friend's telephone number.

Antigone reminded them that she had already told them, on several other occasions, that this girl had no telephone. (On several other occasions, Antigone had already used this girl as an alibi—mostly for innocent outings to the cinema—preferring her for the very reason that she did not possess a telephone.)

The discussion went on for some time, new lies flowering at every step with astonishing facility and profusion. Antigone's father had a great many objections, but he did not quite know how to phrase them: if she had asked to go on a pleasure trip he would have found no difficulty; but she presented the matter under the stern light of the simplest, most obvious of duties. He had always posed as a humanitarian; he could not contradict himself now so openly. Antigone had indeed been clever in her choice of a story.

In the end he gave in, but insisted that her mother should accompany her to the girl's house, as it was after dark.

Her mother was tired, as usual, and impatient at all the fuss. She bustled Antigone into a taxi, and merely drove her up to the girl's door, without even waiting to see her ring the bell (the bell Antigone would not ring). Before driving off, she pressed Antigone's hand: "Don't tell your father we took a taxi. You know how it hurts him to see my money spent carelessly," she said with a small smile.

Antigone pressed her mother's hand back and went off to meet her lover with a warm, tingling feeling of comfort, as if she had shared with her mother not only the sad little conspiracy of the taxi but the more important one of her nocturnal appointment.

When she returned home next morning she dreaded the questions her father would ask; she was afraid she might give herself away. After all, this was her first big lie. Fortunately, he only asked whether her friend was feeling better; and Antigone requested his permission to go and lie down, because she had not got much sleep that night (which was true). She lay on her bed and brooded over the past twelve hours. She could not tell which was most unreal, the night she had spent with Agis, or the night her father thought she had spent with the sick girl. She could not believe she had really done this; what was more, she could not believe that no one knew about it, that it was possible for such an act to be so completely unknown.

But the next time she told an important lie, her fears were much milder, and they steadily decreased with every new lie. Soon, not only did she not evade her father's questions, but she provoked them. She would plague him with long bright accounts of imaginary outings, pursue him with descriptions of imaginary persons. It was as if she were trying to find out how far it could go, the unreality, the absurdity; how soon unreality would give in and prove it was unable to make up a life, a relationship, a family. There were times when she almost expected to wake up one morning and find that he was no longer her father, or that he had become a creature of the imagination, like the people she described to him when she came home after an evening with Agis.

On the ship, he was still the one who kept the accounts. He wrote down every penny they spent; after she had been to the bar to drink a lemonade or some soda-water, he would ask her to bring the notebook with the green marble pattern on the cardboard cover. The question: "How much did it cost?" even took priority over the disciplinary question: "You didn't speak to the currant-merchant, did you?" He also wrote down in the notebook estimates of what they would spend once they got to Zante. He worried considerably. "We don't even know how your mother's cousin will receive us," he said. "And the peasants on the property have grown used to our absence after all these years. Will they be willing to give us our due now?"

He looked at her tenderly: "We are unwanted everywhere."

But in the end he always found a way of comforting himself while retaining the outward form of grief. "After all, nothing very much worse can happen to us now," he would say. “Who will want to harm a broken old man and his child? We won’t ask for much; we won’t be in anybody’s way. We will live so quietly, so humbly, they won’t even notice us. We might even grow happy, just the two of us, without anybody noticing . . .”

He kept the accounts, but there was a difference now; he also kept the money. He carried the wad of banknotes reverently in his breast-pocket, the money which once he had not been allowed to touch. But this did not soothe his pride; it was too late, the harm had been done. He could never be properly proud anymore. As for humility, it was just as problematic; a constant, unstable struggle, like a man who insists on wearing a shoe on the wrong foot. The fact that it hurt made him believe humility had been attained. He mistook discomfort for contrition.

The money in his breast-pocket, finally, only served to remind him of the humiliations he had endured when the money had lain in his wife’s handbag. He went back to this poison again and again. “You will never understand how I felt,” he said to Antigone. “You are a woman—a girl—you will never know. People speak laughingly about the ‘woman wearing the pants’ in the household. It is no laughing matter. It is tragic; it is monstrous, like a hunchback or an albino. It is unnatural. I have a horror of what is unnatural. Being the head of a family is as sacred, in its way, as being a priest. When I begged her for money, I was unnatural; when I demanded it, I was equally unnatural. No matter what I did, I could not be myself. I used all kinds of ruses and devices to get the money I needed from her. And she became extremely inventive in stopping me from having it. She became depraved by the power money gave her; I became depraved by need. One night, when I asked her for money to buy stamps for my correspondence, she said coldly: 'Give me the letters, I will post them for you.' I said I needed some money for several other things as well, adding ironically that I hadn't had time to make a list of them for her. She yawned then, and said, all right, she would give me some money, but not now, she was tired; (her handbag was at her side, within easy reach). She would give it to me sometime tomorrow. . . . Surely you remember that night; it was the time I came to your room, unable to bear her presence any longer. A hideous, unforgettable night. At least, she taught me one thing, the value of money. We will have to be very careful with what we have left, Antigone. We will have to live very simply. You must keep this in mind, when you do our shopping in the village (don't ever send one of the peasants to do it for you), when you visit our tenants, when you talk finances with your mother's cousin in town. I will advise you, of course, as best I can."

He looked at her wonderingly: "Isn't it extraordinary that I should depend on you, my child, so utterly . . . I, who was once . . ." He broke off, smiling, almost amused, almost contemptuous. In spite of his newborn love for Antigone, he still considered her insignificant, puny. She was a product of his; a pure and simple offspring. He could not realise that she now constituted a powerful, independent agency, that this agency had begun to operate on him; he did not know where she was to lead him. He was exclusively paternal. He would have been horrified if he had known that her feelings for him, on the contrary, were more fraternal than filial.

He had no ways of knowing, naturally. Her manner was so deferential. Sometimes she touched his hand; she never went as far as kissing him. The people on deck, the captain, the currant-merchant (he hadn't dared approach her again) stepped aside on her passage, awed by such devotion, such respect. Antigone acknowledged their homage with great poise, with a small dignified smile, at the most. She knew she was not what they believed her to be. But by now, the contradictions of appearances had ceased to puzzle her. Misunderstanding had become a definite, but unimportant, necessity; she had found it need no longer exclude reality.

Antigone had not forgotten the night her father had mentioned, the night he came to her room after an extremely violent quarrel with her mother. She had not forgotten because it had been the first time he had roused some interest in her. After that, there had been a relapse into indifference, alienation; still, she remembered how close they had come to an actual contact.

She had just come home (after a late tutorial, as she had told her parents). She knew nothing about the quarrel; it was all over by then, muffled and crushed behind the door of the parental bedroom. Then he had come staggering out in his pyjamas, and hobbled on his crutches to the threshold of her room. He paused there, closed his naked eyes (his spectacles were off, she had not often seen him like this) and whispered: "Let me stay in your room for a while."

She too was in a state in which he had not often seen her: half-undressed and barefoot. He believed she must be modest in front of all men, including her father. Her calico petticoat was creased, soiled; one strap was torn and had been clumsily fixed with a safety-pin before she left Agis. She hastened to put on her dressing-gown. But he did not seem to notice all this; probably because of his missing spectacles. However, this mutual exposition, denudation (for the first time she noticed he had quite a few grey hairs on his chest and his feet were very white) created a kind of intimacy between them—accompanied by the uneasiness of intimacy.

She helped him into an armchair, the only one in her room. He thanked her, and half-ashamed, said: "I had to come, or I think I would have gone mad. I couldn't lie down on that bed, next to her, and go to sleep, after what happened." They still shared a large double bed, an old-fashioned conjugal fortress.

Antigone sat by his side, silent, her hand on his knee, in the position that was later to become so familiar to them.

"She is lying on the bed, sobbing. A mild touch of hysteria, I should say." But it was clear he was frightened. "Antigone, I hit her."

Antigone woke up; she began asking him questions. Her dull, opaque face became animated.

"I asked her for some money. Her bag was at her side, within easy reach. She said, not now, I am too tired; sometime tomorrow. Then I saw red. The bag was at her side . . ." He told her the whole story. There was shame, there was fear in his face; there were all the symptoms of guilt; Antigone recognised them with a sense of wonderment and elation. She was very close to him now.

He went on, in a low voice: "I shouldn't have hit her. It was an ugly thing to do. I don't think I've ever done it before. But then she had never humiliated me like that before."

"Tell me how you hit her," said Antigone.

But Antigone was to be disappointed. Gradually her eagerness fell, for under her passionate scrutiny, her pressing questions, he soon confessed that he had not hit her very hard, he had merely pushed her so that she fell across the bed. Besides, after the first moment of shock, he was gradually regaining control, and discovered excuses for what he had done. "She drove me mad. She made me lose my head. I cannot describe to you the insolence on her face when she said: 'Tomorrow, you'll just have to wait till tomorrow.' It was more than any man could bear. I have been putting up with these humiliations for so long, Antigone."

This was not true guilt, and Antigone knew it. What was more, perhaps he was right; perhaps there was no reason for guilt; not enough reasons. Her face became patient, weary; she lost interest; she was once more the respectful daughter.

All the same he was a broken man. He lay his old hands on the arms of the chair, he lay his head back.

"If only I could stay here," he murmured. "How am I to go back to that room, how is the long night to pass?" He opened his eyes, that were full of anguish. "Antigone, how am I to spend the rest of my life with her? Face to face, day after day. We cannot separate, or divorce. At our age . . . and she is a good wife, I know it. But how am I to live with her? And when you go away—when you marry—what will my life be in this house?"

Perhaps for him too this night was the first time he really became aware of her, and what it would be like to lose her.

He was on the verge of tears; completely distraught, he begged Antigone: "Let me stay here, let me stay here a little longer. Just a little longer. God, who would have thought it would come to this?"

There was no guilt, but there was grief. Grief remained and it was heavy and difficult to bear. Yet for Antigone it was not sufficient.

She kept him in her room for another hour; she looked after him, made him a cup of camomile tea, wrapped a blanket round his white feet. She was a nurse, a nurse only, and he the stranger who had nearly become a brother. For some people charity can never be completely love.

In her bed that night, after he had gone, a great bitter cry rolled over and over in her, like a wave that cannot break. "Shall I tell you what guilt is like? Shall I tell you what guilt is like?"

She had not known guilt immediately, from the start. Only towards the end, when the circle of deceit grew wider and wider. For she had not deceived her father alone. The lie had been stretched to breaking-point, an arrow tested on many bows.

Antigone had met her lover, Agis, at the chemist's. She visited the chemist's often to get medicine and fresh camomile tea for her father. On most of these visits, Agis had been there too. He obviously came to buy medicine, like her, but he behaved as if the shop belonged to him; he seemed to spend a lot of time in it. She usually found him either weighing himself, like a child, with excitement and concentration, or talking to the chemist, who was perhaps an old friend of his. One morning, when the chemist had gone into his laboratory at the back of the shop to prepare her prescription, Agis spoke to her. Their conversation was dignified and dull. They spoke about illness mainly. They uttered platitudes: "Health is the greatest blessing man can pray for," and "Science has made the most amazing progress in the last few years."

"There is almost no disease that Medicine cannot cure today," she confided to him. "Except my father's . . . I don't believe he will ever get better."

"You never know," he said cheerfully, "they might discover something new, any day now." He was, of course, quite indifferent and unconcerned about her father, she knew it at once for having used that cheerful tone of voice so often herself in her father's presence.

She liked him. He was not very good-looking, his body was thin, almost undeveloped; perhaps he was even a bit shorter than she was. His skin was white, papery, like someone who has lived all his life in a great town of the north. But there was this brightness, this cheerfulness about him.

When he wore his coat (it was the beginning of winter) he looked quite normal, a slight man, but normal. But when he took off his jacket in order to weigh himself, Antigone could see his shoulder-blades sticking out, and the chicken-like thinness of his neck, which had to support a rather large head. She was suddenly taken by a passionate curiosity to see the rest of his body, to see how the signs of manhood would manage to make themselves felt on this infantile body. She had not felt curious about a man's body before—not even, at the age of puberty, about her father's body, so well hidden in the draperies of paternity. Perhaps it was the stillness in the chemist's shop, the ritual of taking off his jacket, which was a beginning of undressing, the stale but delicate smell of sweat coming from his creased shirt. Nor did she feel any repulsion. She came from a dark and stuffy household herself, where illness was considered a necessary evil and fresh air dangerous; a household where fruit was always stewed, a cold shower unheard-of, and a woollen cardigan considered advisable even in the summer months. She had been to an old-fashioned girls' school where athletics were not encouraged, and gym shorts positively forbidden. She had been to the seaside twice in her whole life, and could not swim or ride a bicycle. Her body was heavy, especially at the base, yet no burden to her; she was so unaware of it. She had never felt any attraction for the young, lithe boys who went about the streets in skin-tight jeans, with hard brown chests showing through their unbuttoned shirts, and an elastic spring in their step. They seemed rather ridiculous to her, not quite a part of the real world. Agis, though much older than her, was not only real, but natural.

"Is this medicine for you?" she asked him, when the chemist handed him a small box of pills and two bottles.

"Yes. The doctor says I need some tonics. You can look at them," he said. They stooped over the medicine in silence, like two people sharing a hobby. "I might have to start injections," he concluded with some satisfaction.

It soon became a habit for him to walk with her some of the way when she went home. Not up to her door, because her father might be at the window and he would make a scene. When she explained this to him, he understood at once and did not insist. He even seemed to find it natural.

But when their relationship became more demanding, there was no gradual development for them to follow. As she had no social life, there were no parties, no gatherings at which she could meet him; she had no "gang" of friends which he could join. So from the very start their meetings were furtive, clandestine; nor could there be any pretence that they were meeting for the simple pleasures of friendship. The secrecy, the lies inevitably suggested a more serious motive. In the complete isolation in which she lived, unaware of the life of her generation, in that void where there were no grounds for comparison, in this strict tête-à-tête, there was no other role he could assume but that of a lover. So from the casual conversations at the chemist's and the brief walks back home, they leapt without any intermediary stages to the small basement room which he had rented for the purpose of lovemaking.

When he told her he was married, she was not deterred. It seemed a happy coincidence to her that there should be deception on both sides, rather like the coincidence that they should both be involved with illness. It brought them together. Having lived under oppression all her life, deception was in the nature of things. The fact that he could never marry her, that she would be "wasting her time" with him, did not preoccupy her, for she was no husband-chaser, again as a result of living outside society. She had none of the ambitions of other girls her age, who were governed by different, more competitive laws.

A large part of the time Antigone and Agis spent together was devoted to thinking out the lies they would have to tell after they separated—he to his wife, she to her father. However, it was not long before the lies intended for Agis's wife took up the larger part of their time. Antigone would decide upon the story she would tell her father in five minutes, firmly, without hesitation. One might almost say that she grew careless; her stories were often improbable, or incomplete. It was as if until now she had been testing her father for the position of dupe; his candidature had now proved completely successful; the victory of appearance over reality had been won without a single battle: she lost interest. Sometimes she suspected him of knowing the truth in his secret thoughts but refusing to admit it to himself, because this would force him to put into action an authority which he was quite content to proclaim verbally only. Perhaps he knew that not only with his wife, but with his daughter as well, that authority was a mere shadow and must not be brought out into the daylight of action. Sometimes, when she told her lies, she looked at him straight in the eyes, almost hoping to see the hateful credulity falter. But his eyes remained clear, serene—as abstract as a thinker's behind his owlish spectacles; and her suspicions would disappear before this imperturbable candidness; "he is innocent, innocent, irreparably innocent; no matter what he does he will always be innocent," she would think in despair.

So she didn't bother anymore; her lies to him became simple routine. All her attention was now centred on the lies Agis would tell his wife. Agis was not very good at this, more through laziness, a kind of indifference, than through any fundamental honesty or inability to tell lies. So Antigone's help was invaluable to him. And her inventiveness, inexhaustible. Perhaps she was inspired by the fact that the wife was completely unknown to her. (Agis obstinately refused to say anything about her.) With this absent, faceless victim in the game, the unreality was complete, freedom unlimited; in front of Antigone stretched a great boundless space in which her lies could take flight like bright rapturous birds. No wonder she was intoxicated, and no wonder, too, that she was ruthless with Agis's wife, from the start.

Agis watched her admiringly as she unravelled her bold stories, ever renewed, while he lay limply on the sofa, limply expressing a dutiful compassion for the victim ("Poor woman, if she only knew . . . she doesn't really deserve this, you know"), a concern which, naturally, was too tepid to light any responding spark in Antigone.

These moments of inventiveness, of busy intrigue, were their gayest; perhaps their only gay moments. Antigone's pale face would flush, her eyes become bright, quick, shrewd, and she would suddenly toss back her long dark hair like a burden which she need no longer bear. They would burst out laughing suddenly, and from then on any fresh version of the alibi, any imagined new reaction from the two dupes, became an excuse for uncontrollable fits of laughter; the whole world seemed funny.

Otherwise they were a rather quiet, silent pair. They did not make love very often, because Agis did not always feel up to it; he was very weak, and one day out of two positively ill. Antigone did not mind; she was not particularly sensual. Whether they made love or not, they would sit in their small furnished room, Agis half-reclining on the sofa, Antigone washing the cups they had used the previous time, dusting the bulky, empty, useless chest of drawers, or sitting by his side and stroking his moist palms, a thing which gave him great pleasure. He would only rouse himself from his happy drowsiness to ask Antigone for another cup of Turkish coffee. He never had enough of it, he would drink seven or eight cups in an afternoon. Antigone had grown used to the dry, rather acrid taste of Turkish coffee on his tongue when she kissed him—it was all part of the warmth Agis represented for her, his warm being—just as she had grown used to the faint smell of ether he carried with him after his daily injection, and the continuous delicate sweat that covered him, and the limp white body which she could lift in her arms without the slightest difficulty. All this—the warm, particular being of Agis—bred in her a feeling as intense as desire, but steadier, and stiller, which sought duration, pure, colourless duration, far more than the satisfaction of an outburst. She could burn like this for hours.

Most of Antigone's feelings took this form: a constant, steady concentration, without flashes, without visible light. But there was something indestructible about them.

One morning at the chemist's, Antigone found Agis with a woman. She was holding his coat, neatly folded over her arm, while he weighed himself. She was his wife. When

Agis got off the weighing-machine, taking his time, he pretended he had only just noticed Antigone's presence. He then proceeded immediately to introduce her to his wife, with a slightly repulsive, patronizing nonchalance: "My dear, I want you to meet my 'young friend,'" he said. There was no alternative for him but to introduce her, for the chemist had seen them talking to each other, leaving his shop together, and would have found it strange if he ignored her now.

To Antigone's ears the term "my young friend" and the way in which he said it held something so lewd and leering—a kind of senile lewdness—in its paternal inflexions, that she would have been much less shocked if he had plainly said "my mistress." However, the formula was right, it was what the circumstances demanded; the formula was what mattered most. She had found out that inflexions, expressions of the face—all the things that give life to the formula—were far less important (far less dangerous) than one thought. One thought them important only because when one lied, one was so obsessed with sincerity. And indeed in the fluctuations, the arbitrariness of lying, Antigone was growing much more clearly aware of the nature of the absolute than people who never lie. Duplicity was her apprenticeship for that singlemindedness which was to become her vocation.

Agis's wife was a short, plump creature—not quite a woman, and no longer a girl, though she had a round girlish face. Her manner was diffident, her movements nervous; that was immediately apparent, from the way she shook Antigone's hand. She wore a thick coat, a navy blue scarf; her head was bare. Antigone believed she was not the good-housewife type either; housekeeping, the constant contact with practical matters gave one a kind of assurance, balance. This woman's life must have been divorced from the material world, yet with none of the freedom, the detachment of the abstract. Her emotions were her daily routine, a routine as obsessively monotonous as a morning at the office.

When Agis said goodbye to the chemist and made as if to follow Antigone out in the street as usual, his wife jumped up from her chair and cried out: "Where are you going, dear?" There was no accusation in her voice, not even surprise, only fear. "Get up," said Agis smiling, "we shall walk part of the way together. I think we are all going in the same direction." He was tender to his wife, he was tender to both of them, and he looked very happy. Antigone was absent-minded. Her curiosity—not that it had been very intense—had been satisfied within the first few minutes. Before this meeting, Agis's wife had been a vague figurehead; now she had acquired a form, but she still remained a figurehead, nothing more. There was nothing to be said, nothing to be exchanged, or changed. After her father, her mother, the girl-friend who was supposed to have been operated for appendicitis, the few odd people that she knew, here was one more telegraph-pole planted along her narrow road of life; the very most one could say about these objects was that they gave one a sense of orientation: where to go, where not to go.

When she said good-bye to Agis and his wife, at the street-corner, all she thought was: "Now that I know what she looks like, it won't be so much fun inventing lies for her; but at least I will be able to choose the stories better."

She was a practical person, and efficacy was a positive compensation for lack of freedom. After all, this was no dilettante occupation, no lying for the sake of lying. She never forgot that she had begun to lie because she had to.

But there came a day when Agis's wife actually discovered their relationship; and then the second cycle of lies was closed and a far uglier game began. Antigone found that ruthlessness must be followed to its amazing end; there was no other way—it was in her nature to travel in a straight line.

It had happened like this: Agis said his wife had seen them leaving the little furnished room together one evening. It was stupid of them, they should have left separately. He sounded tired saying this, or rather more indifferent than tired—as if this were no longer his business; as if he knew there was some ultimate protection for him somewhere. He said: "She was not angry, she was frightened; and she wept a lot. I have no idea what her intentions are."

Antigone wondered at this indifference of his. What made him so safe? She tried to imagine what it would have been like if her father had found out instead of the wife: it would surely have meant a great shattering of worlds; yes, the way she had often pictured it, with dread and desire; reality at last marching against appearance, and shattering it; this very thing which she had come to believe impossible. And what would happen afterwards? What would take the place of the shattered forms? Would it be love? Was it true that love could only stand on a ground of truth?

Yet now that there was truth between Agis and his wife, truth between the two women, what had come of it? No destruction or rebirth; simply Agis's final indifference; and Antigone, unswayed, following her ruthlessness to its end.

Against the long green sea, against the long hours of the journey on the deck of the dripping ship, the old man pursued his monologue, while Antigone carried her own thoughts, like a stone, in her closed mind.

They were clear of the mainland, and the sea was rough. Most of the passengers stayed in the smoking-room, playing cards and backgammon, drinking coffee, talking, and finding out whatever shallow mysteries there were to be had about each other. The other mystery—the mystery of the old man and his daughter—remained static. They did not try to do anything more about it. The steward from Zante gave out cryptic, knowing remarks about them, but they did not listen. Curiosity had settled, folded up on a picture that was satisfactory; a loss, a grief, a great devotion. It was enough.

Antigone and her father were the only ones who stayed up on deck after dinner in spite of the weather. Some of the passengers tried to interfere, give advice: "An old man like him—is it wise, my dear? He might catch cold." Antigone lowered her eyes, murmured: "Since he insists . . ." concealing under a show of filial obedience her determination not to shield her father from anything. However, the old man allowed himself to be wrapped in a plaid; but his head he stubbornly kept bare; and received the cold sea spray, with closed eyes and the same tender, happy, wounded face with which he listened to Antigone when she echoed, dutifully, his accusations against himself, the horror of what he had done.

But when night came, their first night at sea, he grew feverish, restless. They slept in the same cabin; it was long, narrow and very hot, for it was next to the engine room. This was the first time they spent a night in the same room. They did not undress. He only took off his thick black tie and his shoes. Antigone took off her dress, and put a black cardigan over her black petticoat. The air was stuffy with illness and old age, the smell of an old man's sweat. Antigone did not sweat because, as usual, she was so still. She watched the high waves squashing themselves against the low porthole of the cabin, a packet of heavy white linen. She listened to the grunts and groans of her father in the bunk below as he tried to turn over in his fitful sleep. At last he cried out, fully awake. Antigone came down to him, found his glasses for him.

"Antigone, Antigone, I can't sleep. It's no use," he said. "Should we have gone away? Should we? Now it seems as if it had happened yesterday. But so much the better. I must not hope to forget, so soon." He gripped her by the arm, as if fearing she might go up to her bunk again.

"Antigone, I haven't told you the whole truth," he groaned. "It's worse than you think. I must tell you the whole truth, so that nothing will stand between us. Love must be grounded on truth. You remember that fatal day; you remember the quarrel I told you about; it was much worse than the quarrel that brought me to your room that other night—the night I hit her. This last time I did not hit her; but it was worse; terrible things were said. I had never hated her so much, and I had never been so helpless in my hatred. In a moment of anger, she tore up all my business correspondence. The correspondence I had been filing so carefully over the past ten years. She said that now perhaps I would be cured of all my foolish ideas, and face reality, and try to make life easier for those who supported me. Yes, she tore up every single letter. This ridiculous correspondence, she said. Then, before leaving for her afternoon lessons, she told me that if I didn't like the way she looked after me, why didn't I go somewhere else? Go somewhere else, she said. Go somewhere else! And there I was pinned to my chair. And the big town all around me, which had grown unknown and alien through my years of illness. And my pockets empty and my wishes meaningless and nothing but necessity crushing in on me, a single force. She left; I remained in the empty house. I wanted to destroy something. How I longed for action! But there was no relief. I waited, and I could hardly breathe. It was only later that I discovered that there is always a possibility for action, even for the prisoner, the slave, the buried.

"You know the rest. How she came back late at night, and rang the bell for she had forgotten her keys. You were out, studying with that friend of yours for your exams. And how she turned away, getting no answer, after what seemed an eternity of ringing, and walked away blindly in the rain. She must have been distraught; her nerves were not as strong as she tried to make us believe—poor household hero; I know how distraught she could get, in her silent, haggard way. And then the murderous avenue. I remember crossing it one day, leaning on your arm, Antigone—once only—when you took me to the hospital for that blood test. I shall never forget it. That steel-coloured desert stretching out, arching a smooth back like a beast, and the madness of the long, low motorcars screaming along it. They never stopped, nothing seemed able to stop them. Nothing between one pavement and the other, not a roundabout, not a road island, not a policeman. The avenue left to itself, screaming mad, all that streaming steel. Yet they did stop; they did stop for an old man limping across on the arm of his daughter. I wouldn't believe it. I didn't dare look; but you said: 'Don't worry, they will stop for us.' And you led me . . . but they didn't stop for your mother, that wet night. She was caught up in all the steel, the blue lights, the rain . . ."

It was no longer the old monologue; he was raving. She did not stop him. She only searched his face, anxiously. "Is this despair? Is this despair, at last?" But after a brief panting silence, he got a grip on himself, caught her arm again, and looked at her straight in the eyes.

"And during that time you thought I was sleeping. Her relatives, everybody, thought I was sleeping, and that was why I didn't answer the door. Antigone, I'm telling you now that I was wide awake. I heard every single peal of that doorbell. This was my way out, my action. All the time she was ringing the bell, I was staring at her bunch of keys, shining on my desk. I had seen them there immediately after she left. I had foreseen it all—except the avenue. But that is no excuse: I sent her out there. That night was my doing, mine alone. You can say that I killed her. Say it. It is true."

He tore off his glasses, fell back on his pillows, exhausted. His eyes were closed, he did not even look at

Antigone, he was so certain she must be appalled by his revelation. She did not tell him that there was nothing new in the story for her; he had told her all this from the very first day, the morning after the accident; and then he had forgotten about it, perhaps because he was old and obsessed, perhaps because he wanted to forget it and then remember it, forget and remember in order to have an opportunity to accuse himself afresh.

"You see, Antigone, I am a criminal," he said opening his eyes, for he believed he had given her enough time to take it all in, and she was now ready for the final certainty, the statement. "Your father is a criminal."

Antigone still did not move. She kept the stony, white, expressionless face which had always been such a great help to her in other circumstances, in the time of the lies; the face in which he loved to lip-read his condemnation.

She was not appalled; not in the least appalled. There was no horror; only pity, grey weary pity at the smallness and the blindness of events, the stupidity of coincidences, the tiny petty actions dragging huge consequences on their backs like unnatural humps; above all, pity for a man who had not been able to conduct his own crime, and clamoured in vain for the fateful hump as his own, his very own.

She turned off the light, but remained at his side. She kept to her difficult silence in the dark, while he tossed and sighed and raved. "I am a criminal," he repeated in a loud, odd whisper, both elated and frightened. She could not bring herself to say "yes," like the first time he had asked confirmation of her, at the beginning of the journey. Nor could she refute him. She could never say: "You are no criminal. It is much simpler. You are a pitiful man who was selfish, ignorant, and had not the gift of dignity."

She thought: Yet it isn't simpler, really. It was the other way round. Crime, pure complete crime was simplest; that was absolute simplicity. With its clear voice, it forced acceptance on one, like orders from above; the humility it brought was unquestioning. Crime had singled her father out, and he was unworthy of it. He had not the stature for it. He must pay not for his crime, but for his ignorance; and the price for that was much higher. Looking down at the floundering old man tossed on those ambiguous tides of remembering and forgetting, accepting and rejecting—looking down on this man who still wanted to live, she wondered how she would ever lead him to the complete despair that had lodged itself so perfectly, like a stone, in her own soul.

But she could not speak. All that she knew now with some certainty—Antigone the justiciary—was that *she* was finished, had been weighed and judged, and that it was this other, imperfect guilt, her father's, that now demanded—deserved—all possible attention, all possible love.

All possible love; the need was urgent. Who dared say it mattered whether a love such as this was grounded upon truth or not?

Antigone could not forget how much kinder guilt had been to her; it had attacked her quickly, with perfect precision, like a hawk; and not till the very end.

After their affair had been discovered, she had not expected to see Agis's wife again; as if the breaking out of truth would exile the woman forever from everyday life, from the common flow, in which one met people, talked, sat down, moved about. The fact that Agis's wife knew about them drove her back into a state of unreality and abstraction; Antigone was not used to the truth.

For this reason she was quite taken aback when she came upon Agis's wife at the chemist's one morning. There was the woman, quite real, sitting anxiously on the edge of a chair. Agis was not with her. She seemed to have been waiting for Antigone. She jumped up when she saw her, then sat down again and turned aside, patiently, politely—but fidgety—till Antigone had received her prescription from the chemist. Then she went up to Antigone and asked her, very nervously, if she had some time to spare, because she would very much like to have a word with her. Antigone nodded obediently and they went out into the street. They were both extremely awkward. Antigone didn't dare speak; she had to remind herself all the time that she could no longer tell lies to this woman; and now there seemed to be nothing else to say.

In front of a rather smart tea-shop, Agis's wife asked Antigone whether she would like to go in and have something. She mumbled some excuse about her house being too far away for them to go there. She did not wait for Antigone's acquiescence, but led her straight into the tea-shop, which was astonishing, if one considered what a timorous creature she was. But the fact that she was in the right and Antigone in the wrong gave her an unconscious assurance.

In the tea-shop, some time went by before they got their order. Here again Agis's wife did not consult Antigone; she ordered, in a low, shy, but unhesitating voice, a quantity of rich creamy cakes; and insisted that Antigone should eat at least three. Antigone felt as if she were being taken out by a distant elderly aunt who still considered her a schoolgirl.

They gorged themselves in sad dreary silence for several minutes. Then Agis's wife drank a big glass of water, wiped her mouth carefully and turned to Antigone; but she did not look up at her.

"Please listen to me, Miss Antigone," she said ceremoniously, in a tone that contrasted ludicrously with the elderly aunt attitude. "Please listen. I am asking you to leave my husband alone."

Faced with the absolute barrenness of this statement, pressed to the wall, Antigone in spite of herself came out with the exact expression of what she was feeling.

"I don't want to leave him," she said bluntly.

Agis's wife stared. She suddenly looked very stupid.

"You have no business with him," she said. "He is a very sick man. And you are a young girl . . ." She let the odd argument trail off, and came back again with: "I am asking you to leave him."

Antigone could only repeat: "I don't want to leave him." She never thought of adding that Agis was the only real thing in her life. There were no excuses, no justifications or explanations on either side. They both sat at their tiny marble-topped table, painfully trapped in their desert of truth.

In order to break the silence, Antigone said: "May I have some more water?"

Agis's wife agreed, with a kind of absent-minded eagerness. She still held her handkerchief (with which she had wiped her cream-smeared mouth) clutched tightly between her fingers, like a sea-sick person on a boat. She said mournfully: "We have been married ten years. I know all about him, all about his illness . . . Life is very difficult . . . So many worries . . ."

"I know. My father is very sick too. He has been an invalid for many years."

Agis's wife asked Antigone a few polite questions about her father.

After another long silence, she turned to Antigone and said (as if she had never heard Antigone's double refusal): "Well, you will leave him alone now, won't you?"

Antigone didn't answer this time. She was quite convinced now that the truth did not lead anywhere. She also realised suddenly—with a certain sense of excitement—that she could just get up and go. There was nothing Agis's wife could do about it.

"But Miss Antigone. . . ." the woman stammered hurriedly when she saw Antigone leaving her chair; and made as if to follow her. But the waiter stopped her, presenting her with the bill. Obediently, shyly, she sat down again to pay it, while Antigone stepped out into the street, head high, limbs free, but her face quite unchanged.

She forgot about Agis's wife very quickly. The only impression the woman had left was a sense of oppressiveness, and this she got rid of at once, as one takes off an old jacket. She knew how to deal with dull, depressing people; most of her parents' friends and relations were of that kind. She had learnt to ignore them, to gaze right through them as she sat in her perfect, self-made vacuum, beyond boredom. In the case of Agis's wife, even her close connection with

Agis had not been able to make her opaque, and real, in Antigone's eyes. The privacy of Antigone's feelings was quite impregnable.

That was not the end of Antigone's dealings with Agis's wife, however. One afternoon, at home, she received a telephone-call from her. The woman was much more eloquent—or rather more garrulous—on the telephone than she had been in the tea-shop. She carried on a hurried, breathless mumble, uninterrupted for several minutes. Once more it was mostly about her husband's illness, mysterious necessities, explanations that explained nothing, strange flat statements that held neither anger nor entreaty. Antigone understood only half the things she said. She hardly said anything herself. For one thing, Agis's wife would not let her put in a word; in the second place, she didn't dare say much because her father was in the next room. She had to pretend it was somebody she didn't know, somebody who was asking for information. She stuck to the safe phrase: "I don't think I can help you." It served both purposes; it was suitable for the ears of both her father and Agis's wife. In this rediscovered ambiguity she felt at home once more, and remained unruffled throughout the telephone conversation.

But Agis's wife telephoned again, not once, but several times. Antigone couldn't very well play the same comedy every time. Her father was growing suspicious. One day, he hobbled up behind Antigone as noiselessly as he could and snatched the receiver from her hands. He jammed it to his ear, saying as an excuse: "Let your father deal with this tiresome person," for he wanted to preserve some semblance of dignity in his actions. Agis's wife, unaware that the receiver had changed hands, went on babbling mournfully along. But Antigone's father was slightly deaf, especially on the telephone; all he was able to understand from the strange sounds which came through was that Antigone's interlocutor was a woman, not the dangerous male he had suspected; and this was all he wanted to know. "My dear lady . . ." he began almost gaily, such was his relief. However, Agis's wife immediately took fright at the sound of a man's voice, and hung up hastily. It suddenly occurred to Antigone that the poor woman had not for one moment thought of reporting the whole matter to her father, which would have been the surest and easiest way of separating Antigone from Agis. It was evident that *she* was in no way prepared to follow her actions to their ruthless end, as Antigone was.

However, though Agis's wife was unable to go to extremes, she persevered in her own stodgy little course, dogged and laborious as an ant. She telephoned again and again. Antigone was slowly becoming exasperated. She never told Agis about the calls; probably because she had omitted to mention the first one, out of repulsion for anything that reminded her of the stubborn, depressing little woman and the awful sterility of their dealings. Besides, Agis's indifference made her suspect that he did not like to be bothered about such things, and that in spite of his serious manner and quiet tastes he was, in his own way, a kind of "good-time man," with all the finished selfishness the term implied. So their small furnished room remained a closed unruffled circle.

But Agis' wife was beginning to lose patience as well; perhaps it would be more correct to say, for a person of her kind: to lose hope. She was in the right; why, then, was nothing happening, why did the girl not understand? She began to realise, slowly and painfully in her dense, slow mind, that there was something invincible in Antigone's phrase: "I am afraid I cannot help you."

So she committed a grave mistake: she appealed to Antigone, she took her into her confidence. On the telephone one afternoon her voice became agitated, conspiratorial. "Listen to me, Miss Antigone," she began as usual, "my husband is very ill." Then there was a break, a silence during which she breathed heavily. Finally she went on: "You don't know how ill he is because he hasn't told you; and he hasn't told you because he doesn't know. Only I know. Shall I tell you what I know? Are you listening to me, Miss Antigone? My husband is very ill, he has leukaemia. Do you know what leukaemia is? He won't be with me much longer. Now we both know, and now you will leave him alone, because I must look after him. What business would you have with a dying man? Illness is the most terrible thing in the world. I know how to look after him. I know what's wrong with him; so you leave him alone and look after your kind father. . . . Life is so difficult. You understand me now."

Antigone only said: "I am sorry. I am very sorry." Once again, the phrase was ambiguous; it could have been meant in a condoling sense; it could also have been the expression of a final refusal. But when she walked away from the telephone that afternoon, her face did not remain unchanged. For once Agis's wife had left a mark.

Antigone felt it most when she saw Agis again. Their evenings together had already undergone a certain change, from the fact that they no longer had to prepare lies for Agis's wife. There were no more fits of gaiety and inspiration; their time passed by silently and uneventfully; not that they were less close for that.

But after Agis's wife had told Antigone that Agis was suffering from leukaemia, their silence became different. Antigone watched Agis. . . . While she prepared his coffee, while he sprawled so indolently on the couch, she watched. She tried to fit the information to him, to place the fatal disease within the frame of that warm, frail body . . . she did not succeed at first. It would not fit. The whole idea broke up into absurd bits, and she had to start again. One evening she took him in her arms and felt a sudden new thrill race through her blood, and found she loved him more intensely, with a kind of anguish which had not been there before. Perhaps that was when she began, at last, to believe in the disease. And then it was done; belief settled in. She knew, and he didn't know. She refused to chatter about medicine anymore. When he weighed himself—so scrupulously—at the chemist's, she turned her eyes away. And in the furnished room, she no longer played about idly with his tubes of pills as she had liked to do when they sat comfortably together. A strange oppression grew in her.

With growing desperation, she came to see that Agis, who had been the only real thing in her life, was now being separated from her by a lie, by the familiar spectre of Appearance. Here too, as with her father, truth had become impossible. She must invent yet another form of pretending. She must see things double once more.

Looking at Agis, she must be plagued by the contradiction: "I know—he does not know. He believes he is ill: I know he will die."

Looking at Agis, she often had bursts of bitter revolt, and thought: "What would it be like if he knew?" For she was unable to bear the inequality between them, and the new distance, where they had been so close.

In this way it is quite possible that her mind had already been long prepared for the reply which she gave Agis's wife the next time she telephoned.

Antigone had blindly thought she would not telephone again, that it was not possible for her to telephone again, there was nothing more to be said after that memorable piece of information. So when she picked up the receiver and heard the well-known voice again, she went dead cold and vibrant, a kind of petrified hysteria; and seeing her father (who had heard the telephone ring) hobble towards her inquisitively, she scaled the last step sweepingly, as if goaded by panic; she whispered into the receiver hastily, but very clearly: "If you don't stop telephoning me, I shall tell Agis the truth about his illness."

Tell Agis the truth. Truth! Never had it been so repulsive; at the same time, never had it tempted her so powerfully.

Agis's wife, speechless, rang off.

The game between Antigone and Agis's wife came to an end a week before her mother got killed in the accident. It ended with a complete catastrophe, leaving a scene bathed in unrelieved ugliness.

After her threat on the telephone, Antigone's blackmail had followed a monotonous, unadventurous course, like most blackmail. Her threats became more and more concise, and her demands more numerous, more exorbitant. Now it was Antigone who telephoned Agis's wife; it was Antigone who insisted that Agis should be left alone; he must be asked no questions if he came back home late; there must be no scenes, even if he stayed away a whole day. If Agis's wife wanted Antigone to keep quiet, she must pay for it by complete self-obliteration. One silence against another. She must cease to exist. Antigone even suggested that she should go away somewhere in the country for a while.

Perhaps she hoped in this way to muffle every trace of the woman's presence and the mortal message it carried, the deadly grey breath, and make the world in the little furnished room whole again. It did not work. Agis remained the tiny incongruous figure which one sees strolling alone, unknowing, at the bottom of a dangerous limelighted arena. Now she hated his indifference, his insouciance. She almost hated him for not knowing; for not knowing the thing she most passionately wished never to have known.

As for Agis's wife she only telephoned at rare intervals now, to beg Antigone to keep her promise, to make sure she could count on one more week of silence.

One afternoon, she telephoned Antigone not to beg for anything, not to make sure of anything, not for any particular purpose, it seemed, except to give vent to a crazy, incoherent flow of grief. The stodgy little voice was frightened and desperate; it had the blind loudness one sometimes hears in children's voices. She sobbed uncontrollably. The only information Antigone was able to gather from her was that she had seen Agis's doctor that morning. There was nothing new, really; only confirmation, only a repetition of the verdict, a reminder of its inevitability. And the strange woman had telephoned Antigone as she would have telephoned her best friend, simply to speak of her grief. "What shall we do, Miss Antigone?" she kept saying, "what shall we do now?" She was unaware of rivalries, enmities, conflicts; there was only death; it was simple.

As Antigone listened to her, she was possessed by a sudden uncontrollable fury; fury against this simplicity of death and its power; against the ease with which it had submerged everything, after all her efforts, covered all the lies, the manoeuvres of a love affair under a sheet of heavy water, so that now it was all one, all death and hopelessness; everything reduced to the single unbearable fact. And fury against this woman who had accepted the fact so completely, and who, in her innocence, had even brought it to Antigone to have her take part in its contemplation.

In bristling silence Antigone listened to the woman's sobbing. Finally, like a person mortally insulted, beside herself, she whispered in a strangled voice: "How dare you . . ." and broke off the communication.

Now she was fully possessed. Hating this truth that had so cruelly mastered her, she must now serve it blindly, spread it like a Gospel, or a disease.

Snatching her coat, Antigone made for the door. Her father was having his siesta and did not hear her leave the house.

Once in the street, she realized she did not know where to go. Her appointment with Agis was not till two hours later. Yet even in her purposelessness, her steps were rapid and clear on the pavement, as she went up one street and down another; so great was the force that drove her. She walked like this for some time; the pace never faltered.

Suddenly she made a sharp turn and headed straight for the chemist's.

Even before she entered the shop, through the glass front, she saw them: Agis and his wife. Behind a yellow pyramid of Kolynos toothpaste, there was the picture, the two heads just showing: Agis looking downward, his wife turned toward him, saying something gentle, her hand about to touch his sleeve. In the background, the chemist's head, at his invisible business. It was a quiet scene. To Antigone it was outrageous, unbearable. She was stifled by this chemical peace that meant nothing, and she must break through. All this was so tangible that she had quick mad dreams of crashing through the mountain of yellow tubes, above which the puppet heads moved. Breaking through, reaching through—to what?

But she merely stepped into the shop, quite slowly. She stood in the middle of it, looking at the two creatures.

It all happened at the same time:

Agis's wife saying: "Miss Antigone, I. . . ."

The chemist saying: "Agis, here's your prescription."

And Antigone saying, crying: "Why do you take all this medicine? What's the use of it? Why do you let them fool you?"

Silence immediately crashed in. Agis's wife, silently, put her hand to her mouth. Agis had his back turned to the two women, in the act of taking his parcel from the counter where the chemist had put it. His hand paused for a moment, as if pinned there by the silence, then it began to creep back once more toward the counter.

Agis snatched his parcel away quickly and slunk out of the shop like a thief.

Antigone leapt after him, reached the door which had hardly had time to close. Through her still muzzled mouth, through her white knuckles, Agis's wife sobbed: "I'll go away tomorrow. I promise you, I promise you."

Antigone soon caught up with Agis. When he saw her come up level with him, he turned and stopped a taxi, still smooth and deft and thief-like, his face showing only the thief's intentness in what he is doing. He tried to slam the taxi-door after him; his arms were thin, muscleless, he did not succeed. The taxi-driver waited patiently for the door to shut before he started. Antigone slipped into the car; without pause she flung to the driver the address of the little furnished room.

Agis crouched in a corner of the seat and went quite passive. Antigone caught his two wrists in an iron grip, and one could not tell, she could not tell, whether this was an attempt to stop him from escaping or a gesture of passion, to take the place of words. Her heart beat deafeningly, and they were like two people dashing off somewhere to make love, paralysed, strangled by desire and impatience.

But once in the room, the two bodies did not come together, the thumping was not eased, the locked passion did not break. Nothing happened. Taking three small steps, Agis went and stood with his face against the wall, and did not speak or move.

Antigone wrenched herself out of the deadlock and moving forward, she brutally grasped his narrow shoulders. She shook him: “Didn’t you hear what I said in the shop? Why don’t you speak? Don’t you want to know? Or do you know already? You’ve got to speak to me!”

No sound came from the slight, erect body. She shook him, and told him. She cried the strange spiky word: leukaemia, several times, at the turned back. She shouted at the top of her voice, as if to convince herself that she was not merely echoing the dreadful voice on the telephone, the inexorable decision. Perhaps she even thought she had made the decision; she was the killer; for that was preferable to blind necessity.

Agis let himself be shaken, a creature filled with sawdust. He kept his face to the wall. The frail, bird’s shoulder-blades were beautifully flexible in her strong hands, they cried for destruction.

At last he turned round. It was the same passive face. Yet not the same; he was shut away now in an indifference far more formidable than any he had shown until then; the rapturous indifference of a man occupied with his own death; at last fully occupied, fully given over.

He moved away from the wall. He did not listen to a word she said.

Antigone struggled with all her strength; she shouted, she begged, she battered herself against this incomprehensible thing, this wreckage which truth had made. Unhearing, he crossed the room and said lightly: “I must go home now. Goodbye, goodbye.”

She stretched out her hands; he was gone; there was nothing; it was as if her hands had never touched him, they were so empty. This was what death meant. This was Agis's death. And it belonged to her, cupped in her own two empty hands.

It was her awakening; swift and precise like a hawk attacking. It stamped out all that had gone before. There was only Agis's face—pale, entranced, horrifying, even though it was perhaps a happy face in its final indifference. The evil of that scene stood out all by itself, naked, divorced of past and future. It would never be absorbed by life, by all the things that transform human actions as they are lived out. This evil was indigestible as stone.

So this was the finishing-point—hideous in its desolation. She tried to turn away from it but could not. There was nothing else. She was left alone with herself; and she hated herself completely. She thought with horror of the long years ahead living in this company. She considered killing herself; yet that peculiar sense of justice in her finally made her reject the idea of suicide; she did not believe herself worthy of it. In the end, with a great flat despair, a beginning of the deadening that was to come, she decided she would have to endure herself, carry the act along like a stone, without hate, without love, without much thought even, simply holding it and knowing it was hers.

It was in this still, frozen state that her mother's accident found her.

On the morning of her mother's death, Antigone stepped out of the shadows and came to life; for she had been as if dead during the week that preceded the accident.

She had not known her mother did not sleep in the house that night; she had come home quite late and found the place in darkness, which had seemed natural at the time.

But in the morning there had been the strange furtive presence of her father in the kitchen preparing his own breakfast. As a rule, her mother did this for him. He was eating it silently, huddled in a chair at the cold kitchen table, in the grey kitchen light, like a beggar eating a crust of bread on a doorstep.

When she asked him where her mother was, he looked up at her almost in fear and said: "She is not here. I don't know where she is. I don't know what has happened to her." She realized at once, with a shock of recognition, that he was not telling her the whole truth. He knew more than he admitted. At last the roles were reversed, and she suddenly found him down, down at her own level.

She asked him why he had not called her, so that she might prepare his breakfast for him. He turned his face away and muttered that he had not wanted to disturb her. That too was a lie, but the strange new humility behind it was genuine.

Then there had been the telephone-call from the police station, announcing the accident.

He had not broken down at the news; on the contrary. He emerged from his shrunken, shifting posture, and suddenly assumed the stark simplicity of a man standing against a wall. "I did it," he said at once. "I locked her out last night. We had a bad quarrel." He was shaking very badly, from head to toe, but there was nothing degrading about this, no more than there would have been in a man shaking with a high temperature. Antigone tried to make him sit down in his old armchair; but he leaned with all his weight on his walking-stick against the wall, and refused to move. His mouth was dry, Antigone saw him swallowing several times, very fast. She tried to support him; their hands met. He grasped her fingers and held them very tightly, with a strength she had not suspected in him, and looked at her wildly, nakedly, full in the face. Antigone returned the gaze passionately. Her heart thumped hard, as though in front of a precipice. This was the first time in their whole lives that they were looking at each other.

The police wanted Antigone to come and identify the body. They said the father's presence was not necessary—one relative was enough. But the old man wanted to go with her; he said so tentatively, questioningly, as if asking Antigone's permission, or her guidance. She gave it without hesitation, with loving thoroughness: "Yes, you must come," she said. She would spare him nothing. She was passionate and ruthless; as ruthless as she had been to herself, after the final scene with Agis, when she knew she was finished, weighed, judged. They were together now; her father had come to her, in the horror of this death, which he had caused; and of the other death. There was no call for pity, because they were together, they were one. Pity implies distance. Pity separates. They belong to the same family; the blood bond was now strong, level, and direct.

She did not accuse him, and she did not sympathise with him, even after they had seen the mutilated body; simply, she was with him. It was Antigone's most absolute moment. All her past lies and divisions resolved themselves in this extraordinary communion. Her apprenticeship was completed. The swarming, sprouting lies had brought out this one perfect blossom.

At first, her father said he had been asleep when his wife rang the doorbell. But as if infected by Antigone's ruthlessness, he followed the trail of his crime to its dark end and soon confessed the whole truth. He had not been asleep; he had heard the bell, he had deliberately locked her out. At the end of his confession, Antigone was there to receive him, in perfect readiness. She took her place in his life.

When Antigone saw her father standing against the wall, more horrified than frightened, hating what was done and could not be undone, she thought she recognized all that she had been through herself. It was like coming back, from a cold and distant death, into a room filled with people. So there were others; there was one other, as close to her as one could possibly be; a father and a brother. Closer than the indifferent, invulnerable Agis had ever been. Her exile was over. That was why she was able to suggest, with such ease, their actual exile to the island. They were both already cut away from the world; yet together they were a world in themselves. So they must keep to it, make it as separate as possible.

Her father was surprised, he had not thought of this solution. They had not visited the island for many years. The property had never yielded much.

"There is nothing for us here now, in this town," said Antigone. And she meant it. She thought that the main reason she was taking her father away was that she could no longer see Agis. Agis was gone from her, gone, snapped away, worse than dead; perhaps dead. There was nothing to keep her in town. It was her astonishing, almost inhuman humility that made her invent this selfish motive. She hardly dared admit the strange new devotion to her father, out of humility, out of shyness, too. She was very shy with him at first. She had never been demonstrative, and this great change between them only made her clumsier than usual. He did not notice; a certain reserve was part of what he believed filial behaviour should be.

Clumsily, shyly, but firmly as well, she insisted about the island. He must come. There was no other way. In persuading him she was helped by this inner compulsion of hers, pointing toward the island. Blindly she longed for the dead quiet, the finality they would find there. Finality not for herself; for her father. Because he had left everything incomplete, unfinished. She knew it now: her father lagged behind; he wavered, he suffered, he was alive; this was not guilt as she knew it. The fraternity she had glimpsed on the morning of the accident was not to be, not yet. Perhaps it would never be. Still, his crime must be finished off for him, in the quiet and finality of the island. One does not go back, one does not hope to go back after such acts, said Antigone the justiciary. The guilty mess would be burnt clean, cleared of pity, of his all too human clamours. Then he would be able to rest with her.

She took her place by his side, by the wheelchair on the ship, not knowing yet how inexorable she would prove to be: for she would spare him nothing. She would lead him to her own complete despair; to the place of rest which was at the same time the place where the Furies live.

•

One by one, Antigone's ship left the little obscure ports on its itinerary behind it. The onlookers along the narrow piers gazed up, tiny, at the tall, tall ship, and were gradually lost from sight, a group of dumb people forgotten in a pit. Now the ship was nearing the last port. Nobody seemed pleased to be arriving. The passengers gathered their belongings with a sigh, and were ready much too early. The food had steadily grown worse, as they ran out of cheese, fresh meat, butter. The stewards had become indifferent and neglected to shave, leaving that for their first night ashore. The cows, which had been unloaded on one of the previous islands, left behind an odd feeling of emptiness. The captain seemed to be sulking; this had been his dullest crossing, as far as passengers were concerned. Nor was there anything to look forward to once they arrived. "God-forsaken places," he muttered, "why do people go on living in them?"

The currant-merchant kept asking Antigone: "Why are you going to that awful island? A young girl like you—you should be going to parties, and walks in the park . . . Look at me. I'm only going there for business, I'll get out as soon as I possibly can. Next week, probably. How long are you going to stay?"

"We'll stay as long as we can," said Antigone.

"Perhaps you will allow me to offer you an ice cream on the square, one of these evenings," he suggested with extreme politeness. He respected her.

"We shall not be living in the town. We have a small house in the country, several miles away," said Antigone.

"Why should they want to go and live in the country?" said one of the stewards to the captain. He was the steward who came from Antigone's island, the last island. He was a steward now: a man with a salary and a uniform, a man who had travelled a great deal, and he looked down on the affairs of his native island with contempt. "Those peasants," he sniffed, "the peasants from the village where their house is—well, they're not going to like having those two there. They hate their guts. They're all Communists, anyway. All these years, no one ever thought of visiting the property. The peasants let the goats loose in the vineyards, they've drained the wells, they use the olive-trees for firewood. They've been very comfortable! And now these two come along. An old imbecile in second childhood and a girl, a mere child . . . they must be crazy. Who's going to bring them water, vegetables, eggs, who will work for them? Life isn't going to be easy for them, I can tell you that. I know those damn peasants well . . ."

But the captain had lost interest. "Can't you see they're as poor as Job?" he cried impatiently. "If anything, they're lucky they still have a house there." And he dismissed the steward.

The story got around. Sniffing and shrugging, the steward carried it about like a bad-tempered prophet. The house, it seemed, was not even fit to be lived in. The peasants had put their hens in it. And the owners of the neighbouring property had been forced to leave, the peasants had made life so impossible for them. Somebody asked: "Is there a telephone in the village? Can they communicate with the town, if necessary?" The currant-merchant was much concerned. "That village is no place for you. Why don't you stay in town?" he begged Antigone. "There is a little hotel, it is very cheap. Believe me . . ."

"That house is the only place we can go," said Antigone.

Her father was only hazily aware of the talk that was going on. He did not ask for details. Once or twice, he made as if to address the steward from Zante, but did not dare. So he merely smiled at him, uncertainly, very timidly, a rehearsal for his future attempts to make friends with the islanders. All he said to Antigone was: "Is it going to be very bad over there?"

"Yes," said Antigone.

He nodded and closed his eyes, baring his face once more to the sea wind.

He seemed to grow gentler as they drew near their destination. At the same time, the passengers grew kinder to him, the pity in their eyes more obvious; it was like a conspiracy of kindness on the eve of an execution. They spoke to him occasionally, they offered him oranges, some even invited him to come and see them when they reached the island. He thanked them very humbly and profusely, and refused everything. "You are too kind," he kept saying, "you are too kind." And he meant it.

"They should not be so kind," he complained to Antigone sadly, "they should not be kind to a man like me, how am I to explain that to them? Besides, I am no longer in a position to return their kindnesses. I am no longer what I used to be . . . In the old days, I was somebody on this island, Antigone. You don't remember. And then your mother's cousin will soon tell them who I am, what I have done. Do you think he will do that? Still, let us spare them the embarrassment of our acquaintance. These good people have no business with us . . ."

He looked at Antigone wonderingly. "My poor child, what am I doing to you, what am I doing to your life? How is it you don't hate me? But you didn't hate me even after I killed your mother. It is the innocence in you."

She gazed back at him mutely and very nearly sighed, very nearly envied him for his freedom to talk, to confess, to let his grief remain fluid. She had only her carved life, and that stone in her.

But Antigone had ceased to make comparisons. All she did now was wait for the day when they would fall silent together. She would never tell her father about Agis, about that other death. The two guilts must always run parallel; they could not meet. But one day they would come and lie quite close, almost touching. Hooded love would sit still, and there would be silence and peace; peace without understanding.

When the ship entered the harbour at high noon, it was assailed by a horde of vociferating porters who had come in motor-boats and sailing-boats; the waters were too shallow for the ship to come alongside. Soon the lower deck was a seething mass of people. "You will *have* to let me help you," said the currant-merchant to Antigone, almost angrily. "Can't you see what's going on here? We'll have to lower the wheelchair gently, very gently . . ."

Antigone said: "Very well. Do as you wish." She had a vague look; she was gazing out at the flat shadowless harbour where the boats would take the passengers. The light was very white and dull. The tiny, squat houses stared. Her father accepted the currant-merchant's help silently; his objections seemed to have disappeared; at the end of the journey kindness did not matter anymore. He too had his eyes fixed on the harbour.

A man in a dark suit came up the gangway. He wore a collarless shirt. His face was gaunt, unshaven, the colour of steel. It was the relative, the cousin of Antigone's mother. He pushed the people aside coldly. "So you've come," he said to Antigone and the old man. "Is that all the luggage you have?" He smiled down at it, amused.

"We don't need much," stammered the old man.

The cousin smiled again, insolently. "Good." Then he turned to Antigone. "Come along now, it will be some job getting *him* down."

He moved off briskly; he pushed the protesting currant-merchant aside, gave some orders. He asked for the ropes which had been used to unload the cows. "But the gangway . . ." spluttered the currant-merchant.

"It's too narrow. This is no liner. This is no seaside resort," the cousin said. "So what do you want? What do you want anyway?" Once again he had a vastly amused smile. "He'll be all right. Watch and see."

The old man seemed to panic for a moment. He searched desperately for one face in the crowd—the face of the steward from the island. When he found it, he questioned it, appealed mutely. But the steward, brooding and detached, refused to take back a single one of his prophecies; refused all hope. Then the old man turned to Antigone. She said nothing.

The porters looped the old man up deftly, wheelchair and all, in the thick knotted ropes, like a bundle, like a cow, while the cousin shouted out his cool, savage orders. The first-class passengers made way for him, forgot to hurry. For a moment, the wheelchair dangled ludicrously in mid-air. Up on deck, the captain watched sullenly. Antigone followed.

THE RETURN

For the fifth time that month Eugenia wrote to her brother:

"I can't stand it any longer. It is getting worse. What have I done to deserve this? You think I'm exaggerating. Don't you? No, I don't really know *what* you think. You never write. It is all very well for you, living far away in a big and wonderful place, among good, wonderful, cultured people. It is easy for you. No, no, forgive me. I am thankful that you at least have been spared all this filth. You will lead a good life; you will be clean, good and famous. Out of this miserable family, you will survive; and you are all that is worth surviving. As for us, the sooner we are forgotten the better. Forget us. Never come back."

She thought the letter was finished. Another part of her secretly knew it was only interrupted, and made her withhold her signature. The heroic attitude of the closing phrase was gratifying, but impossible to keep up. Next day a post-scriptum cropped up to put things back in their natural place.

"And yet—what will become of me if you don't come back? Ever since you left, I have been dreaming of the day you would come back and put everything right. I shouldn't dream like this—but I must, I must. You are all I've got. Whenever I am not thinking of you, I feel the dirt crawling on my skin, closing over me—I am finished. It's like living in a stable, a cow-shed; hot, damp, thick with stench; and all the animals crowded together, nudging, pushing, treading on each other's feet, rubbing their dirty wool together, breathing each other's breath, shuffling in each other's filth. I suffocate! What can I do? How can I get out?

"Alone I can do nothing. That woman is invincible. Because she has no memory. Every morning she starts her filthy life anew, with the same dreadful zest, no matter what horrors may have taken place the night before. I tell you, she has no memory. So perhaps it is true the past has gone out of her mind completely, as if it had never been; perhaps it is true she feels no remorse. Yet I can't quite believe it. Won't I ever see her broken, beaten, or simply—ashamed? Only you can do that. Do you know she hasn't mentioned you once since you left? Yet she can't have forgotten her own son . . ."

Eugenia's mother fumbled in the crowded kitchen-sink for the coffee-pot. The sink was stopped, so that dishes, pots, pans, glasses and one enormous frying-pan swam about half-submerged in the brown water that filled it. They bumped gently against each other as she fished out the coffee-pot, unwashed like the rest. She simply emptied it of the brown liquid and began to make coffee. She didn't bother to open the windows; she wasn't properly awake; besides she was too fat and could not push the shutters back far enough. While the water boiled, she went into the dining-room to get some cups. It was dark, like the kitchen, and very stuffy, the windows hermetically closed against the cold. The air smelt of the sour breath of Eugenia, sleeping heavily on the dining-room sofa. Trying not to make any noise, her mother's hands became like butter, clumsier than usual in their awful overripe softness. The cups were stacked on the sideboard, behind a row of small bottles of sticky liqueur; banana, peppermint and creme de cacao. There was a crash; two of the bottles were upset and the cups, liberated, toppled forward.

Eugenia woke up. She woke up like a thief, or a soldier, with a great start and a series of hoarse cries and grunts. Clutching the bedclothes to herself in a lump, she looked around the dark room haggardly. Her mother pretended not to notice; her hands went on moving uselessly among the cups, patting them, pushing them softly, coaxing them half-heartedly into order, looking very busy and deft but achieving nothing. Eugenia spotted her at once, the bright pink satin shining by the dark sideboard. She was up like a shot, in her nightgown, and pounced—yellow duster-like flannel against pink satin. Screams spurted out of the darkness. Eugenia screamed with fury, her mother in fear and entreaty, but both voices sounded alike and were equally loud. Eugenia wanted to throw her mother out of the room; Eugenia clamoured for a bedroom of her own: Eugenia, the victim, claimed for herself the right not denied to the poorest of the poor, the right to sleep.

"Only in sleep can I forget you. And you want to take it away from me. Do you understand?" she said, her voice dropping level at last, but still quite loud. Her mother, deafened and excited by her own screaming, the way children are, kept it up. She babbled out implorations, endearments, lamentations indiscriminately; and following the same quick pattering rhythm, her fingers hooked themselves on the blazing yellow flannel towering above her, only to be as quickly unhooked by Eugenia. Eventually, she noticed how silence had set on her daughter's face; and switched off her screaming instantly. In a matter-of-fact voice, worried, she said: "You must be mad, you've surely woken him up with your screaming."

Eugenia was about to flare up again; when a whining, sleep-thickened voice came to find them from the adjoining room.

"Nini! Nini! Aren't you going to bring me my coffee?"

"Yes, my love, at once, at once."

The crumpled pink satin was quickly gathered up from the darkness, and she bustled away to the kitchen with the cups pressed against her bosom.

Once again Eugenia was left planted there with her huge ridiculous anger, like a silly tree caught in a stretch of asphalt pavement. Somnambulistically she trailed back to her sofa and began to fold the bedclothes. The blanket was the one used to cover the ironing-board; the dirt in it had hardened with the hot pressure of the iron; and it was marked in several places with fin-shaped burns. She put the cushions (which she used as pillows) back in their faded crocheted cases. And then? The useless hungry creature drifted into the kitchen; she could not leave anyone, or herself, alone.

From the doorway her dead, deaf voice said: "Tomorrow I shall move to the sewing-room. I insist on having a room of my own. It is my right." Her mother answered exuberantly: "Darling, of course!" The tone was loud and inexpressive, like bad brass. "You could even move in today, except that the little dressmaker is coming this morning to mend the sheets. But tomorrow, of course, why not?"

The ease with which the promise was given showed how often it had been repeated, and devaluated. Eugenia nodded regally, accepting the false gift out of vanity. One final stroke, to complete what she considered her victory: "Of course you never dreamed of making a cup for me. Aren't I supposed to drink coffee like other people?"

Madame Nini gave her a cup, and without receiving, or expecting, any thanks, hurried away with the other cup to the bedroom.

At eleven o'clock, with all the windows opened at last, the squalor of the house was laid bare, like a teeming anthill under a boulder.

In the sewing-room the little seamstress was already encamped among the paraphernalia of her trade. She had a small body and a rather large head, with sandy hair and pale eyes; her legs were swollen from so much sitting, and her hands tiny. She was a precocious-looking creature, would always look precocious no matter her age. She knew everything; she had tremendous assurance. Her voice was never raised. The smile of reasonableness never left her face.

She had an insatiable desire to put her knowingness to use; she disguised this as a need to be helpful, so as not to be too much disliked.

"Dear Madame Nini! Please let me do it, don't tire yourself," said the little seamstress as she saw Madame Nini smothered in the billows of a mended sheet which she was trying to fold.

"There. Aren't I here to help you?" She was not the only one who was pretending. Madame Nini's inefficiency disguised a laziness—the laziness of the utterly selfish.

"Oh, oh," puffed Madame Nini, "there goes the bell. Have they begun coming already?"

"Madame Nini, you must forgive me. That must be my little niece . . . I have taken the liberty to ask her to come here. She is learning to be a dressmaker like me, that is her great ambition, and I have promised to show her how to do buttonholes today. There was no other time . . . Do you mind very much? I'll make her help us with the hems, and she can help you in the kitchen too, if you like."

"Martha is in the kitchen, I think," Madame Nini said vaguely. "I must go and see . . ."

The dressmaker's niece was let in. A skinny, yellow little girl of twelve. The moment she got in she proudly put on a pair of felt slippers and fastened a little bag of pins to her breast—the insignia of the dressmaker.

The front door had just been closed when the bell rang again. This time it was two older girls in bright coats. They sat in the dining-room very demurely, as if they were visiting at some great, noble house. But they kept their coats on, for the stove had not been lit yet. They showed great deference to Madame Nini, who spoke to them indifferently, as if she did not quite remember who they were, but acknowledged their right to be there.

The travesty of dignity went on for some time among the debris, among the small Oriental tables inlaid with mother-o'-pearl, clotted dust and crumbs; among the ashtrays filled with old olive-stones; the carpet filigreed with stray threads and broken toothpicks; Madame Nini's cosmetics, lying among the liqueur bottles on the sideboard; her box of Tokalon face-powder, her great salmon-pink powder-puff, dotted with small grey clots of dirt in the fluff; the hairpins in the saucers; the stockings, the bright underwear on the coat-hanger, among shopping-bags and handbags and hats. When Madame Nini had visitors, she flung her best silk kimono over the coat hanger, so that all one could see was the kimono, as if blown up with air, standing by itself, headless, against the wall. But the girls were not quite visitors, like most of the people who crowded the house in the daytime. Attendants, acolytes, disciples, that was the kind of air they wore. In reality they were either relations, or people who considered Madame Nini their benefactress (nobody knew why), and who, out of gratitude, wished to offer—or sell—services.

In the kitchen Martha the hunchback was preparing the food of the dead. In a big cauldron she stirred the boiled wheat, the parsley and mint and almonds, the grains of pomegranate, the cinnamon and the golden currants. The result would be a dazzling, festive platter, a dish of fairyland—the humble brown wheat coated with snowy sugar, silver dots, the pink dash of pomegranate, candles. Madame Nini would carry this platter to church, triumphantly, at the commemorative service for the repose of the soul of some dead relation or friend. On the way neighbours would stop her and cry out: "Beautiful, beautiful! Only Martha can make such beautiful kolyva!" After the ceremony, the guests swallowed their portion of kolyva out of small individual paper bags, comfortably mixing pleasure and lament. "May his soul rest in peace," they said with their mouths full.

In the dining-room Madame Nini put her hands to her yellow hair and addressed the two girls appealingly: "And I haven't even thought of what we're going to have for lunch!"

The girls murmured sympathetically:

"Poor Madame Nini!"

"How you tire yourself, how you torment yourself!" "Martha. . . ." pleaded Madame Nini, "Martha . . . Martha. . . ."

Martha was deaf. One of the girls slipped into the kitchen and tapped the steam-crowned hunchback on the shoulder, Martha came and stood at the door, dazed, with her dripping ladle, her monstrous, bristly ugliness.

"Martha, what shall we eat?" cried Madame Nini.

"I'm busy, I'm finishing the kolyva," mumbled the hunchback.

"Have you thrown away the broth in which you boiled the wheat?" Madame Nini asked her sharply.

"No . . ."

"Then throw in some macaroni . . . Or rice? Macaroni. And tomatoes . . . and onions . . . you know. You hear, Martha?"

After she had gone, the two girls purred like cats, like pigeons.

"What a good cook you have, Madame Nini!"

"She is not my cook . . . She only comes in for the kolyva. I have no one, no one . . ." she looked distracted. She had lost her cigarettes.

From the adjoining room came the same whining voice that had asked for coffee earlier that morning.

"Nini . . . Nini . . . aren't the kolyva ready yet? Give me a plate of them, I've been smelling them all morning . . ."

"Yes, my love, at once," she sang. And the girls whispered and lowered their eyes and said: "How is the dear Reverend this morning?"

"How do you expect him to be? So many worries, so much work . . . Ah, you don't know what a man he is. A holy man, a holy man, I tell you!"

Madame Nini was in the kitchen getting some kolyva for her lover when the bell rang again. One of the bright girls slipped into the kitchen to tell her.

"Who is it? Who is it?" She tightened the pink satin around her body, but it had no shape, never would. "Is it the fortune-teller?"

"It is a nun," whispered the girl. "Her name is Fevronia, and she has come for the Reverend."

After a long whispered discussion it was decided the two girls would continue their visit in the sewing-room with the seamstress and her niece; Madama Nini would join them later after having helped the Reverend to dress. Martha would make Turkish coffee for everyone in between kolyva and macaroni. As Madame Nini hurried away to her lover, she warned the girls: "Keep your coffee-cups, turn them upside down . . . Martha, make the coffee thick, with plenty of dregs . . . the fortune-teller will be here any moment. She's coming for me, but I'll tell her to read your cups as well."

And the hunchback was left alone again, among the wet fumes that brought out the smell of vegetables rotting in the dustbin. Almost alone, because Eugenia was still there, sitting unnoticed, ignored, like a beggar-prophet, at the kitchen-table. Absorbed in her thoughts, she munched some bread. When Madame Nini and the girls had left, she suddenly burst out laughing.

"The Reverend! Did you hear that? He is no more reverend than you or me. Where's his church? Where's his parish? Where are his robes? Just because he has long hair . . . That's only because he's too lazy to cut it. They're all lazy in this house, lazy and dirty and sloppy. And the way they all kiss his hand! He pretends to be modest about it, he withdraws his hand, ever so gently . . . but it's always there, that filthy hand, within easy reach, spread out on his stomach casually, you know, all ready to be kissed! One day I will spit on it—I swear! I will bow my head, as they all do, the worms—I will reach out for that hand, very nicely, very sweetly, reverently—I know how, I've seen them do it, he can't resist it—and then I'll spit on it! Bite it! No, spit, spit, spit—And then I'll tell him. I've a lot to tell him. I'll say I'm not taken in by that phony religious magazine they're publishing. 'The Voice of the Lamb'! Ha! I know what's behind it. I know whom that voice is calling! You don't realise, they could go to prison for that. Easily! But if it were only that . . . No one knows, no one suspects. Sometimes I think I'm dreaming. She smiles so much, she weeps so much, she's so soft—I can't get at her. I can do nothing. No one would suspect . . . Even you don't believe me. Nobody believes me. Nobody listens. But if you only knew! Prison is too good for them, prison is nothing. It wouldn't change anything. She would still hold court there, still smiling and weeping, sloppy and soft, and the girls would come, and the unfrocked priests would come, his equals, his little brothers, and he, he—he would cross his hands and be the Martyr. And she would show him to the worms that surround her, to the jailers and the prison walls, 'look at the holy man,' she would say—shameless, shameless. . . ."

She put her head on the wooden table, among the breadcrumbs, and sobbed; tired out with hatred and impotence; dry, sterile, going through the awful repetitive routine of sterile suffering, like a rheumatic having his daily fit, his daily dose of pain. When she recovered, she lifted a dry, tired face and rested, as after heavy work. Then she picked up her pointless day where she had left it.

The sewing-room was humming with talk and the whirr of the sewing-machine. A lean wolf watching a campfire, the figure of Eugenia hovered outside the room.

The women saw her and called her in. She went to them at once, saying she needed the ironing-board. The fortune-teller presided, a little fat, tidy woman holding a coffee-cup between delicately arched fingers, uttering quiet prophecies. The girls' eyes were brighter than ever, their lips too, licked over and over again in their suspense. Even the little niece had her dreams, and waited patiently for her turn to hear them uttered by another's mouth, beautifully codified. They all sat crowded on a large, ancient bed, except for the dressmaker, who sat by the machine.

"Miss Eugenia," said the obliging dressmaker, "come and have your fortune told. I'm sure you must have a very exciting cup."

"Yes, my love, have your fortune told," repeated Madame Nini obediently.

Eugenia turned slowly. A light came into her dull eyes. "I don't need to have my fortune told. I can tell fortunes myself."

A chorus of delight, entreaty, coaxing. And in the midst of it Eugenia blushing triumphant, coming to life irresistibly. She had rested, she was in perfect form now.

"Very well. We shall begin," she cried, "with the lady of the house." And she took Madame Nini's cup from her.

The fortune-teller smiled politely.

"Now let me see," said Eugenia jubilantly, "what have we here? A letter, a long letter. . . . No, it is not a letter. It is a visit. A tall stranger from very far away. I can see the seas that separate you—dark seas . . . He is very fair, even fairer than you. His name begins with a . . . a P. No, it is an O. His name begins with an O. He is coming soon, soon. In three days, three weeks, or three months. There is a great joy and a great sorrow."

"Which will come first?" asked one of the girls slyly.

"They will come together," said Eugenia. "This is a very crowded cup; it is tangled like a forest. . . . Many things grow in it. Long ago, in the very beginning (there, at the bottom of the cup) there was a clearing, a big clean space. But the forest has grown all around. . . . People, many people . . . occupations, papers, money. . . ."

"Is there a lot of money?" asked one girl, and Madame Nini, who had remained silent, repeated the question with her eyes, eloquently.

"A lot of money," said Eugenia sternly. She would not dwell on it. She went on: "And there is a great door. . . ."

"A ministry?" said the dressmaker.

"A palace," breathed the little niece.

"A bank, a church, a prison, it might be anything," said Eugenia lightly. "But no, let me see . . . the great door is blocked. There is that O again. He is in the way. And from him stems a thread, a road, a chain that leads to . . . I can't see, there is a black patch. This is the darkest place of the forest, it is so dark that I can't see. . . ."

"Martha made the coffee too thick," Madame Nini said fretfully, "I told her to be careful. When she's making kolyva she's hopeless!"

"It's quite true, my cup is full of dark patches too," the dressmaker said helpfully.

"It is the position of the patches that matter, not what caused them," Eugenia said sententiously. They were silenced; even the professional fortune-teller had to nod in assent.

"Of course, you may call it a clot, if you like. I can only say what I see: darkness, utter darkness, like the blackest cloud, the blackest night, like ink, like blood. But don't worry too much, perhaps it only stands for a widow's weeds. . . ."

Madame Nini went pale; the others hastily crossed themselves. The sewing-machine was dead silent. She had them completely now; paralysed, subjugated, full of awe; and all horribly tempted to taste the dark unfamiliar fruit of Eugenia's prophesying after the sweetnesses of the professional fortune-teller. They had all felt, at one time or another, that strange, secret little pinch of disappointment upon returning from a fortune-teller who had satisfied their dreams too well, confirmed their hopes too completely.

Shamefully, the professional fortune-teller turned to Madame Nini: "I have often seen that dark patch in your cup. But I didn't want to tell you, so as not to upset you."

Still falsely cheerful, clinging hard to her assurance, the dressmaker said: "Please have a look at my cup, Miss Eugenia. There are two black patches, much darker than Madame Nini's. . . ."

Eugenia gave in. She was already so intoxicated that she did not need much coaxing. She read all their cups, growing more inspired with each cup. Her cheeks were flushed, the words came easy and lively from her mouth. She knew how to talk to them, what expressions to use, vivid and a little vulgar, gossipy and Biblical. She was one of them. The air was full of sisterliness; it was like a girls' dormitory, a convent, a sweaty dressing-room after a women's basket-ball match. As Eugenia read her cup, one of the girls slipped her arm round her shoulder, without thinking.

Eugenia forgot so completely why she had originally taken up the game of fortune-telling that when her mother, her target, got up to leave the room, all she felt was disappointment at the thought that the party was breaking up.

The two girls shook minute threads and pins from their coats, patted their hair. "Is it already one o'clock? Impossible! . . ."

Madame Nini's voice was heard in the hall begging the nun Fevronia to let her come and spend a week at the convent guest-house. She was badly in need of rest, peace. . . .

The dressmaker hustled off her little niece to buy a spool of white thread for Madame Nini's sheets. In the coffee-cups that lay scattered on the bed, the spilt dregs grew cold and sticky. Eugenia was left empty-handed, dazed.

With the usual tactlessness of people too anxious to please, the dressmaker said: "That was wonderful, Miss Eugenia. You really gave us something!"

Eugenia looked at her without answering. She was uneasy. She got up and left the enemy camp in a hurry, much too late of course, since it was now deserted.

Feeling the need to punish herself, she hardly ate any lunch. Besides, Martha's macaroni was uneatable; slimy with grease, and the tomato sauce watery. The Reverend had still not left his room; now he was having a private conference with a lawyer. Madame Nini ate her macaroni with sad, unconscious gluttony, pushing her food on to her fork with great swabs of bread. She interrupted herself once or twice to beg Eugenia shrilly, through smeared lips, to eat up her food and not to make her life a misery. Martha ate with them, silently and methodically.

People continued to drop in. Eugenia's plate of cold macaroni was offered to each of them in turn; the fourth visitor accepted it. The others sat around the soiled table and had cheese, a few wrinkled olives, some liqueur.

Though Eugenia was not eating, she did not leave the table. She sat there stolidly, listening and watching like a hawk, interrupting the conversation at times with a rude remark. Sometimes she laughed to herself, perhaps to prove she was detached, on her own.

"At the beginning, long ago, there was a clearing, a big clean space. . . . That was very good," she thought. Then quickly she turned her attention back to the conversation. She mustn't miss a word. It was her duty to be here, to mix with the worms. She was the observer, the sacred spy, the sentinel.

The porter's wife appeared at the door, wrapped in a black shawl. Madame Nini did not ask her to sit at the table like the other visitors, but hurried her off into the kitchen. A few minutes later, finding an easy excuse Eugenia picked up an empty dish and went softly toward the kitchen. On the kitchen table there was a glass of water, and the porter's wife was very carefully pouring drops of oil in it from a bottle. Madame Nini, her back turned to the door, stooped over her and spoke urgently: "I've been wanting you to come and exorcize us for days . . . never found the time . . . so many things on my mind . . . It's her, I tell you, I'm sure of it. . . . Her evil eye, you can tell at once. Everything's going wrong. I feel ill, deep inside me, here, business is bad, and the Reverend can't sleep at night. . . ."

The porter's wife nodded slowly, and went on pouring the ritualistic drops.

A quarrel had broken out in the dining-room. Somebody banged a fist on the table. Wine was spilt. Martha did not bother to clear up the mess, she went on chewing her food; she had given up working for the day. The Reverend half-opened the bedroom door and closed it quickly again. In the sewing-room the little niece was sobbing, because the dressmaker had told her to go home. Eugenia wandered about. The house was full, chock full, every room of it; in every room, there were people, there was talking and breathing, plotting and friction, till the air was thick with it all. Eugenia reeled a little, like someone gasping for breath, or if one looked closer, like someone drunk.

The evenings were quieter. The lamps were lit, bedside lamps with heavy velvet shades, long fringes. The dust became a silver bloom, the untidiness became organized by the pattern of the shadows; the squalor grew intimate and warm, encrusted on the night like smoky, leprous bronze. The kitchen was abandoned, given up as hopeless till the morning came again to expose it. Madame Nini did all the evening cooking on a tiny spirit-stove in her bedroom; not much cooking: mostly warming up left-overs or a plate of food from the neighbouring restaurant, and making tea from herbs; lime-tea, mint and camomile.

At dusk, Madame Nini disappeared in the bathroom for hours; she emerged, unbelievable butterfly, in her gaudiest kimonos, negligés, housegowns, her face freshly painted. Now her many duties were over, now, she said, she could be a woman.

Sometimes she would push the bedroom door, leaving it slightly ajar, and love games followed in the big, red-lamped room. She was the kind who giggled and laughed while making love. Other times they sang psalms together. When the Reverend was not feeling well, Madame Nini played patience.

Through the warm, homely, brothel-like air of Madame Nini's world Eugenia circled like a maladjusted eunuch.

Gleaming dimly on the dining-room table Eugenia saw the kolyva Martha had prepared, spread out on an enormous tray, beautifully decorated, silvery and snow-white, a fairy cake, immaterial, not to be touched. She glanced through the open bedroom door; Madame Nini sat in front of her dressing-table, carefully painting her toe-nails among her silken draperies. She bit her lips and grunted, for her big belly made it difficult for her to reach her feet. In the double bed, the Reverend lay wrapped up in Madame Nini's blue angora bedjacket, like the wolf in Red Riding Hood. He was reading a newspaper.

As usual Eugenia felt a strong urge to destroy the peaceful scene. But today she was satisfied with herself. At lunch she had been magnificent. In spite of this apparent calm, her mother must still be smarting under her hints, her poisoned well-aimed shafts. So she smiled.

"Who are the kolyva for this time?" She was almost indulgent.

Silk rustled. The grunting grew heavier, forced. Eugenia appeared at the bedroom door. "Well, who are they for?"

There was a mumble. "You must be joking . . . you know very well who they are for . . . didn't Martha tell you?"

Madame Nini looked around desperately for the corn ointment.

"No, I don't know," said Eugenia, dead serious. For a moment her anguished face looked as if it didn't want to hear any more.

"They're for your father of course . . . Isn't it a year since. . . ."

Eugenia stepped swiftly forward. She put her hand, almost gently, on her mother's shoulder.

"But my father's not dead," she said, slightly suffocating. "How dare you make kolyva for him?"

"Oh, Eugenia, why must you always. . ." cried Madame Nini.

"You have no proof he is dead," Eugenia went on, still aghast, white-lipped, "it's not written down anywhere that he is dead, is it? he was just missing, missing in the war, that doesn't mean dead. . ."

"If he were only missing," said Madame Nini quite logically, flickering back to her practical self, "why hasn't he shown up? Why hasn't he given us any sign, all these months?"

Eugenia shouted: "That is none of your business! What are you talking about? Signs! You don't need signs. It is not difficult to believe. It is not difficult for a wife to believe her husband is not dead! There are no papers; there was no announcement, no official from the Government came to you to say he is dead. No one in the whole world could say with certainty: this man is dead. The word was not spoken. Yet you are the first one to say it! You have tried to make him dead! You refused to report his absence—shut up—you refused to report for investigations—you even refused to listen to the messages on the wireless. You didn't try to find him. You didn't want to find him. Once I liked to think you did it because you were afraid to be told that he *is* dead. But no! You only wanted to pile up silence on him, bury him in silence since you couldn't bury him with your own hands!"

"You don't understand," gasped Madame Nini, "the death duties . . . I couldn't report his absence, they'd have got at me, you don't know what death duties are, we'd have been ruined, in the streets . . . don't forget I had to feed you, keep ourselves alive . . . two miserable women, alone in the world. . . Eugenia, you know I was never good at formalities, filling in forms and all that. . ."

"The kolyva!" thundered Eugenia. "The kolyva! Are they formalities too?"

She brought the tray and pushed it into her mother's face. She became violent, ludicrous; plunged her hands into the beautiful fairy snow and thrust handfuls of it into Madame Nini's mouth. The fat woman ran round the room barefooted, her fat feet half-painted and spattered with sugar, her silk draperies pulled above the knee. In the feathery feminine bed the Wolf turned to the wall, covered his face in his hands and whimpered: "An aspirin, an aspirin!"

Madame Nini suddenly turned aggressive. She got back her healthy temper. The whining, ingratiating tone, the trembling, the entreaties which she used only because she was so soft, so lazy, too lazy to shout and hit back, were peeled off like a layer of fat, leaving her free, strong, lively. She got hold of Eugenia and shook her; then looking at her straight in the face, jubilating, she frankly cursed the day she had given birth to her. She was more impatient than angry. Certainly she could return none of the fierce hatred that contorted Eugenia's face. The warm pink brothel-room, devastated, the sensuous family peace broken, her nails half-painted, Martha's masterpiece spoilt—all because of this stubborn, ugly obstacle standing in the middle of the room. Push her away, brush her off, discard her! Out of the way!

"Get out!" she bellowed, expulsing her voice as if the sheer strength of it could sweep Eugenia out of her sight.

"I will get out," said Eugenia in a strangled voice. "At once. Tonight."

Madame Nini shrugged insolently, her vulgarity fully deployed. This was not the first time Eugenia threatened to leave the house. She had never carried out her threat. But this time, she did.

There were not many places where she could go. She had no friends. She rarely left the house. The only people she saw were her mother's acolytes. Her life had been lived out in utter, maniacal concentration within the narrow confines of her self-chosen prison, her spy's hunting-ground. The outer world did not exist.

There was just one possible person: a distant cousin of her father's, a stern elderly woman living alone on a pension at the other end of the town. Her name was also Eugenia. Since the death—or disappearance—of Eugenia's father, she no longer visited at his widow's house. She disapproved of Madame Nini. Not enough to go and seek a quarrel or bring her to shame in her house; but selfishly, joylessly, from a distance. She was a selfish, joyless woman. She was so like Eugenia's father that she could have been his sister.

Her house was situated in an entirely different quarter than Madame Nini's, not more prosperous but more respectable. It stood on a broad, straight new avenue with yellow trolley-cars going up and down it. There was no market on Fridays; there was no lively bustle of shops, peddlers with their wheelbarrows, barbers shops open till late at night, ablaze with fights; there were no taverns or cinema. To justify so many negative qualities, the prim, smug inhabitants liked to call their district "residential."

Eugenia was awed when she entered her aunt's house. So awed that she forgot to sob, to vent her hatred, her disgust and despair in her aunt's arms. It was better like this, because the old woman would not have liked it.

It was not prosperity that awed Eugenia, for there was none; her aunt was perhaps even poorer than Madame Nini; but the cleanliness, the tidiness. She had become so used to the squalor in her mother's house that the scrubbed red tiles on the floor, the stiff plastic table-cloth dazzled her more than parquet and lace would have done.

"What a wonderful housewife you are!" she exclaimed to her aunt. "How do you manage to keep it up, all by yourself? Ah! I remember," she added bitterly, "now I remember, our house looked like this too, when my father was with us."

The house—a flat in a modern block—was so tidy that it seemed empty. Nothing was allowed to lie about. There were no signs of cooking in the cold extinguished kitchen, no imprints of human bodies on the well blown-up, uncreased cushions in the armchairs. There weren't even any pictures on the walls, perhaps so as not to make marks on them. The electric bulbs hanging from the ceiling were bare, for lamp-shades gather dust and must be avoided. There was no ash in the ashtrays, no flowers in the flower bowls. When the old woman made a cup of coffee for her niece, the traces of the crime were instantly removed.

Eugenia admired everything. She sat on the edge of chairs, her feet drawn together, and nodded again and again. "This is the way to live," she kept saying, "this is the way we used to live. . ." The sight of her aunt's house awoke in her a strange nostalgia, not so much for her father, but for the lost respectability he had stood for; and also a sad envy, a pathetic spirit of competition, as if she were begging admission to this clean world, this closed, correct world, on the grounds of a long-ago membership.

"Do you remember, Father used to insist on the ash-trays being emptied after the third cigarette. He was very strict: no more than three cigarettes in every ashtray. And he was making allowances, you know! Because he didn't approve of smoking in the first place. . ."

Later on she said: "The fuss he made if he discovered dust on the furniture! That is the gesture I remember most clearly about him: the way he rubbed his forefinger on the top of a chest or a table, and then looked at it carefully. . . . He was so thorough, so methodical. The Army taught him to be that way. A lifetime in the army, that is the best training. *She* was terrified of him. Of course we had a maid in those days, it was easier. There was even a time, I think, when we had two maids. . ."

Her memories became more and more splendid as they unfolded.

"Do you remember the day his Colonel came to dinner? Everything was perfect; he saw to everything; he inspected all the table linen beforehand, and discarded three tablecloths before he found one that he considered suitable. The Colonel was so impressed. He even said something—some wonderful compliment—what was it? Anyway it was quite clear he had never been entertained like that before. And *she*—she took all the credit for it, simpered and smirked, while my father—what dignity he had! you remember? he simply bowed very slightly without saying a word. . . ."

In the midst of beatitude, memory deviated and brought other images, and her face was gripped with anguish. She leaned forward:

"Aunt, Aunt—if you saw where we live now! If you saw the people who visit us now!"

But although the old woman was willing to put Eugenia up, glad to receive her, she did not have much sympathy with her predicament. She did not understand it.

"It was silly to run away like that," she said, mending minute holes in a piece of lace curtain. "You didn't have to run away. You don't even have to live in that house. Why don't you go to work, a lot of girls do nowadays. Then you can find a place of your own to live. If you hate the woman so much, why do you stay with her, why do you eat her food? I dislike her too, and I keep away from her. That's all. It's only sensible. Or you might join your brother? His scholarship isn't expiring for some time, is it? He would surely be willing to look after you."

Eugenia went pale. "No, no, I can't join him. I must not. He is building up a fine career over there, what would he do with a poor creature like me? Everybody at the university says he is going to be the best engineer they ever had. He doesn't say so, he is so modest, so reticent, but I can guess. I would only be a burden to him. Perhaps I would even embarrass him, shame him in the eyes of all those fine university people—the way I've become. . . . He is so handsome and clean and upright. Like my father. Whereas I . . . look at me; don't pretend. I know. It's all those months living with her, in that filth—But perhaps he will come back one day, soon. He promised he would. And he must find me there. I can't go away and let her wallow in her filth alone, undisturbed. You don't understand, Aunt, you don't know! I am the thorn in her flesh! I poison her life. She says so herself, every day. Do you know something! She even brought in the porter's wife to exorcise the house from my evil influence!"

She was exulting. She had not only a justification; but glory, glory of martyrdom and sacrifice; the mere obscure sentinel had grown into a defender of the faith. She whispered, huge with secrets, with hidden powers:

"She is afraid of me. Just as she was afraid of my father. So you can imagine what it will be when Orestes comes back. She will faint, dissolve, fall on her knees. . . . She doesn't even dare mention his name, Aunt! She is right; even I do not dare think what Orestes will do."

They ate in the kitchen; the meagre food of old people or convalescents—boiled potatoes and rusks and yoghourt. It was as if even in her choice of food the elder Eugenia was guided by the thought of what would soil her pans least. After washing up, she asked Eugenia to forgive her, but she must go to bed. She always rose early, for she had many things to do. She advised her niece to follow her example; she must have had a tiring day.

Eugenia's sacred exaltation had fallen. She had been silent throughout the meal. But she was not sleepy. The great upsurge of feeling remained suspended in her, in a no man's land. Confessions, reminiscences, the flow of words was no longer enough. She needed violence—like an addict; the daily dose so faithfully provided by Madame Nini.

She prowled round the house, not daring to touch anything or sit down. There were no newspapers or books. There were no sordid women's magazines for the spy to censure. There were no closed doors behind which to eavesdrop. She looked out of the window in the perennial posture of all prisoners, but the avenue was bare like a rod of steel, and the shops far away.

Her bed waited for her, with clean sheets and a new blanket, such as she hadn't seen for months. She looked at it admiringly and regretfully, as if knowing it would only be hers for a night. Then she sat down dutifully at the dressing-table, and began a letter to her brother.

"Out of the fullness of my heart I write to you—you have been so much in my thoughts today, in the kind house, the good house of our dear father's Cousin Eugenia. . . ."

It was not quite true. Orestes was no longer in her thoughts. If the truth must be faced, she was lonely. And if it were faced even further, she was bored.

•

She went back home next day. She straightened her shoulders as she said goodbye to her aunt. "They must not be left to themselves," she said. "I must go back. Give me your blessing."

The old woman shrugged ironically. "As you wish. If you think you must. . . . But they'll drive you crazy in that house, if you don't watch out."

"It won't be for long. My brother will come soon and put everything in order. I am waiting for my brother," she said heroically. Then dropping the plaster cast of nobility, she flashed out full of appetite: "Meanwhile, I'll make their life hell."

She did not take the trolley-bus. All she carried was a bulging schoolgirl's satchel, which she had taken instead of a suitcase. She went the slow way, walking, stopping, looking around. Her eyes were dreamy, she talked a little to herself as she went. But the rest of her was so ordinary—the old navy blue coat, the heavy unattractive face—that no one stared, or even noticed. As she left the grey, flat quarter where her aunt lived and approached the vulgar heart of the town, the commercial travellers' hotels, the gaudy early cinemas frequented by loafers, the steaming coffee-shops, a mounting exuberance bulged in her heart, and she walked more rapidly. "Is it because I am frightened of going back?" she wondered. "I feel strange—drunk! Perhaps it's true they're driving me crazy. What is all this?" She looked left right, left and right—the white lights, the red lights—she looked all around till the lights merged into one circle. The noise of the traffic was like the sea. "I'd like to dance! All by myself. Touching the ground with my hands, round and round on a beaten floor." She remembered that near her mother's house there was a restaurant with a courtyard, and a few trees, and a gramophone standing on a table by the door, an old shrill gramophone with a yellow horn. From the kitchen window, one could often hear it at night. The music came in with the smell of food. Then in the surrounding houses, one could see other kitchen windows lighted up, and framed within them, still and standardised like ikons, the white faces of scullery maids fixed at the eternal sink, washing dishes, listening too.

She was still some way off from home. But she wasn't afraid of getting lost. She knew her steps would inevitably take her there in the end. She passed a shop that sold women's underwear; she stopped because a general dominating pinkness in the window—salmon pink, peach pink—caught her eye, and because the colour was familiar. She laughed sarcastically as she remembered Madame Nini's flowery bedroom trousseau. At the same time she thought wistfully that if she had been a good mother, it would have been nice to buy her a present—a new corset? a petticoat? a pair of garters, the ones with forget-me-nots on them? Surprise and pleasure. . . . She corrected herself angrily: if she were a good mother, she wouldn't wear such gaudy things.

It was getting late, dark. Instead of closing, the shops seemed to open wider, turn on more lights, in order to receive a sudden onflow of late customers. In first-floor offices, people lingered on to talk after work; outsiders dropped in; coffee was offered, windows opened for a hand to reach down for the evening papers. Cars purred against the kerb, arriving, leaving, and taxis began to prowl. Everybody was getting ready: to finish, to begin. And Eugenia among them, also getting ready, for what she didn't know—didn't stop to think; she was on her way. She imagined splendid scenes: Madame Nini revelling at her absence—a kind of horrible banquet, something between lovemaking with wine and guests present (the "girls," the nuns, the porter's wife), and a religious thanksgiving service, with the Reverend officiating, just out of bed—nasal psalm-singing and a grain of incense burning in a chipped ashtray. Among them would come the dark Eugenia, the owl that brings bad luck, the bird of doom, Jesus in the temple, the ghost, by proxy, of her father (but I am not like him, she thought in distress, not like him at all. Orestes, he is like my father, the very image of him. Only he will be no ghost . . .)! She cheered up. All would be well; there would be justice, punishment, blood; she hurried towards the hated house as toward a place of fulfilment.

There was a big scene; but not as she had expected it. Her mother was prepared for her. She had not been revelling; she was too occupied by fury. The Reverend was more prostrate than ever.

Madame Nini sat in state in the drawing-room, surrounded by her whispering, cajoling acolytes, like a matriarch in mourning. Between cups of camomile tea she told them about the pain of being a mother. It was not mere literature; she was also worried about her future. "What will become of me when I am old? She will throw me out of the house; she will turn me into the streets. She is heartless, heartless. And the Reverend won't last much longer, with all these worries. . . ."

When Eugenia appeared, Madame Nini let out such a hair-raising howl that the women sprang forward to hold her to her seat, expecting the worst. There were no preliminaries this time, no wheedling and victimizing; Madame Nini had had ample time in which to work herself up; and Eugenia was riding on the crest of a wave. In the same breath, with perfect synchronisation, they addressed each other as whores.

Then Madame Nini screamed: "Where did you spend the night? Where? How many men? Where?"

"How dare you ask me that," Eugenia panted, "you of all people."

"You're no better than me. You're my flesh and blood," Madame Nini screamed deliriously, and Eugenia, fighting desperately against the hot breath on her face, the hot soft hands that dragged her down into the thick blood bondage, gradually felt herself sinking, sinking, outraged, exhausted, and almost happy. At this point, with the same wonderful timing, both women simultaneously burst into loud sobs, and they were finally parted and led to separate rooms by the eager acolytes.

Her brother's arrival the next day took her all the more by surprise as the violent scene had left her sated, quite content to wait another long spell for an arrival that had become mythical.

There must have been a letter from him announcing his arrival. There had been a letter, and Madame Nini had intercepted it. But not read it; she was too superstitious for that, too superstitious even to tear it up, for that would be an outrage—not to the human rights of privacy, but to what had been decreed, written, done and not to be undone. Instead she hid it away in darkness, muffled it in her darkest drawer, under old underwear, where perhaps it could no longer act; gentle coaxing oblivion instead of destruction.

Orestes did not appear as Eugenia had imagined: a flaming angel at the door in the middle of the night. He sent her a note to say he was staying at a neighbouring hotel, and would she meet him there.

But her emotion couldn't have been stronger even if he had appeared suddenly at the door. Alone with the little piece of paper, the mysterious summons—like an oracle from a God—the miracle gripped her. It was some time before she could get up and walk. In her empty bloodless heart, happiness lurched achingly like a ship at sea. When the blood returned to her body, she wanted to shout the news; not so much to her mother, not as a threat—but to the whole world, in triumph and pride: simply that she had a brother, and that he had come for her. She had someone at last, someone of her own, who had come and who cared. When Madame Nini asked her, amazed, where she was going, she said nothing about her great appointment. She was all taken up by happiness; she could not be bothered to use the miraculous news as an instrument of punishment; not now; she refused to be distracted. But she had time for a small taunt, a side smile as she left: "I am going to meet a man," she answered.

Madame Nini was about to start shouting at her; but she felt tired and soft again after last night; and in the flat light of the morning she realised with kind contempt how improbable it was that Eugenia should have slept with men the night she ran away.

"Come now," she said gently, "stay at home, be a good girl. Haven't you made enough trouble? Don't go doing anything foolish. Stay at home and I'll cook some nice halva with almonds for you."

Eugenia laughed out loud at the bribe (which in other circumstances she might have accepted), so tiny, so ridiculous in front of the great joy that awaited her—and left quickly.

Her brother was unpacking in his room. She ran to him, and cried like a little girl in his arms. She stroked his cheek, his hair, looking up at him dumbly. He was utterly unlike her; tall, very blond, with a clean, clear skin, a smell of soap about him, glass-clear eyes, perfect white teeth. He did not quite know how to take her silent adoration. He was evidently moved, and a little embarrassed. When they were children, she had always been the bossy sister, not like this. Besides, he had just arrived from a country where people prided themselves in their self-control. But he was moved; perhaps also flattered. As he continued to unpack, he glanced at her often, and smiled reassuringly.

She only found her usual petulance again to scold him for having come to such a shabby hotel. "If I had known," she said, "I would never have allowed it. Don't forget you have a great career ahead of you, a reputation to think of, you can't just go anywhere. If anybody saw you here!" She already imagined him illustrious, his name known in all the great capitals.

"I wanted to be near you," he explained. "And then you don't want me spending all my money on taxis coming to see you, do you?" He smiled, indicating it was only a joke. It was not quite; he had taken from his father a certain thriftiness, a concealed carefulness about money. "Besides, I won't be staying here long."

She didn't dare ask him what he meant, what were his plans. Instead she shook herself from her trance and offered to help him. But he was extremely tidy and efficient, and the job was almost done. Her crude, timid hands on the edge of the suitcase, she contemplated the clothes, the brushes, the shoes that belonged to him and that were no longer the things she had seen him growing up in. "Where's your blue tie?" she asked. "And what's happened to the lovely thick white socks Aunt Eugenia knitted for you? Don't tell me you've thrown them away!" As if he had only left a month ago. He smiled again, without answering. But she was not thrown aback or depressed by the disappearance of all the familiar identification marks. On the contrary, she was thrilled. Everything about him was new and wonderful. He was a stranger who was her brother—beautiful contradiction; he was a stranger yet not forbidden, or indifferent; she knew his name, she could utter his name while touching his unknown sleeve.

"The only trouble about this hotel," he said thoughtfully, "is that they won't take in my laundry. So I wonder if you. . . ."

She hardly let him finish, she began hunting round the room for the linen he had not yet soiled. She remembered now, even as a boy—and it was unusual at that age—he had an obsession about clean shirts; he had to change shirts at least twice a day; worse than a "gentleman." She used to laugh at him. Now he was a gentleman, and she was a miserable nothing, and his wishes must be followed religiously.

He snapped the empty suitcase shut and put it away. He turned to Eugenia: "Now," he said, "Let's talk. So our mother is now living with this man—this false priest, is she?"

"You mustn't call her mother," she said hotly. "I never do, never."

"At least," said Orestes, raising his eyebrows, "she could marry him, she needn't flaunt their liaison like this, with a grown-up daughter in the house."

"She daren't marry him," said Eugenia triumphantly. "She is not a widow yet. Nobody has said Father is dead. She pretends he is, she hides all memory of him away, the way she hides the letters she steals from me. But she doesn't know—nobody knows whether my father is dead or alive."

Orestes went on methodically: "There has been no sign of him since I left?"

"Nothing. Nothing. . . . Sometimes, God forgive me, even I stopped waiting for him. And I began waiting for you. . . ."

"You haven't made any further inquiries?"

"I tried. . . . It was so complicated. I didn't know where to go. I am so ignorant, stupid! At one place they asked me many questions, they asked for all sorts of papers, birth certificate, army certificate. . . . I had nothing, nothing. She said she hadn't got any of his papers, he had them all with him. Sometimes I thought even they did not believe me. I also tried listening to the wireless, to the Red Cross messages. Names, names, my head would spin with names. . . . Then she had the wireless put out of order. I swear it was her! She pretended to be upset, she even accused me of breaking it, because I used it so often. She gave it away to be repaired, she said. They never brought it back. And now it is too late; perhaps there are no more messages, after all this time."

"Yes," he sighed, "yes. Though I suppose if he really wanted to, he could have found you, even though you moved to another house. . . ."

"Perhaps he *didn't* want to," she said, pouncing eagerly on the possible explanation. "Perhaps he knows it, feels it, wherever he is. That she has wished him dead, in his house, in his bed, in his family."

Orestes shook his head. "She never loved him. It was one of those stupid marriages. But since he was her husband, she should at least have mourned for him a little. But our mother was always a selfish, empty-headed woman."

Eugenia wasn't really listening to him. From the depths of those two long years, grief welled up; and up floated the humiliations, raw as new, the neglect, the hardships; the scenes that made a beast of her, so that she no longer recognized herself. The feeling of trudging in warm mud and never breaking clean again—

"Sometimes it comes to blows. She pulls my hair, she screams at me, and I feel terrible things in my mind. I feel I want to kill her. But when she is in a good mood it is worse. I can't bear her, the way she sits there flowering out like a horrible fat plant, quite, quite happy—And she says nice things to me; she calls me darling, 'I'll make you some halva, darling,' she says; but she's only trying to get something out of me; she's always trying to make me do things for her. She even makes me wash her—soiled underwear (if you can call it underwear!). All this in front of her 'friends,' in front of all the disgusting people who crowd that house as if it were a brothel. Then she lies back in her bed and says with a sigh: 'Thank God and all the saints. Safe this time. I had a feeling I was pregnant again.' She is so proud of still being a 'woman'! She brags about it every month, she misses no opportunity of mentioning she is 'indisposed.' And the awful women smile, and pat her on the back and tell her she must rest. . . . Do you understand now? Do you? Orestes, Orestes!"

He smiled at her cry, but only as in a parenthesis, then he went on with his questionnaire, gentle, puzzled:

"But who are these awful women you keep talking about? Who are all these people? I don't suppose she has kept up with any of our old family friends, has she?"

Eugenia dropped the dramatic tone and turned eagerly to direct, practical attack. She made him sit beside her. She told him about the clandestine magazine, the strange comings and goings, the shabby lawyers, the girls. Her voice came in a sharp, fast whisper, her hand gripped his arm. "Perhaps the place is a brothel after all, a secret one. . . . All those girls! She procures them. . . . Or perhaps she sends them to doctors. . . . They are so grateful to her! Why are they so grateful?"

Orestes listened attentively. He seemed much more interested in this information than in anything she had said before. "We shall have to look into this," he said, pressing his lips with decision. He asked her more questions. Eugenia answered eagerly, obediently, like a soldier. Obscurely she sensed that she had captured his attention now, his whole attention, and that her previous outburst had perhaps been only a monologue. Humble, she did not mind how she got this attention, what it was that drew him to her, as long as he was there, turning his serious, important face to her. Later she would speak freely once more; she would ride her misery again like a wind in front of him. And he would come to understand everything; and he would no longer be gentle, but passionate, and frighten her with a hatred stronger even than hers. This was only the beginning. There was time.

Orestes sighed again and said: "Well, we shall see. Now I must write some letters—you don't mind?"

"To whom?" she asked, curious without shame.

"To some people you don't know," he said with a smile that was a lesson in discretion.

"Aren't you going to have lunch?"

"I had my lunch before you came. Having lunch early is a bad habit I have picked up abroad. . . ."

This time the foreignness about him did not thrill her so much; it gave her a small pinch of fear, fear of never reaching him, out there in his bright new world.

"Will you come back later and take me to the house? Or would you rather stay here while I finish my letters?"

"I'll come back later," she said timidly. At the door she clasped him silently in her arms and left.

She waited two hours before going back to him, and they seemed endless. She thought first of going back home and getting started on Orestes's shirts, but somehow she did not dare. She couldn't face her mother now; she was shaking all over, it was as if she had lost the centre of herself. She did not know where to go; she had nowhere to go. Whenever she thought of going home—which had once seemed so natural—the house appeared in her mind like a closed facade; she couldn't see into it, couldn't see herself in it. Now that Orestes had come, it was not only impossible to go there, but also mysteriously forbidden.

In the other direction, the hotel, Orestes, the future, were not ready for her. She wandered aimlessly between the two buildings, the house and the hotel, grey and unsubstantial, a ghost of herself. She thought: "It's as if I hadn't been born yet." Then the hope, the happiness rushed back into her blood: "Orestes will bring me back into the world. He will give me a new life, and make a new being of me." And she turned toward the hotel again, trembling, as if to undergo an operation.

She ushered him into the house nervously, almost on tiptoe—like a girl bringing her lover home for the first time.

Madame Nini emerged from the bedroom whining: "Who is it again?" Setting eyes on Orestes she let out one short, piercing scream, and Eugenia regained confidence. "Here is your son," she said coolly.

Madame Nini rushed forward, her draperies in a turmoil. She showered Orestes with tears and loud kisses, which he neither repulsed nor returned. He seemed to be waiting, exquisitely polite and patient. His fairness shone in the dingy room like something precious. At his side, Eugenia was once again adoring and proud.

When Madame Nini showed signs of having nearly spent herself, Orestes took her by the elbow and said: "Let us sit down now; we must talk."

He was treated like a guest, and did not seem to find it unnatural. The blue kimono was hastily thrown over the coat-hanger; ashtrays were quickly emptied into flower vases, the doors revealing the infamies of kitchen and bedroom were closed. Madame Nini patted a few cushions, and then her hair. So she has felt the foreignness too, thought Eugenia, too pleased with her mother's panic to feel degraded by the similarity of their reactions.

Madame Nini gave Eugenia a sharp meaningful glance and mouthed the word "coffee." But when Eugenia had prepared it and set it before him, he would not touch it, excusing himself with charming formality. Eugenia's face fell; she felt oddly hurt at his refusal. Then she noticed his clear blue eye fixed on a trace of old lipstick round the edge of the cup. It was Madame Nini's lipstick, Eugenia never wore any. Yet instead of feeling relieved of responsibility, her sense of slight grew even more intense. Her face burned dark with shame, she was on the brink of tears. Without quite knowing what she was doing, she suddenly picked up the cup and said brusquely: "All right, don't drink it. I'll have it." Her mother looked at her surprised. Eugenia seldom drank coffee at this hour. She turned back to her son sweetly: "A little glass of liqueur? Oh, please!"

But Orestes had decided it was time to put frivolities aside. He began to question his mother. The questions were tactful but very thorough. He hardly ever looked at her or Eugenia; but kept his eyes on an invisible notebook on his knee. Most of his questions were about money; what had she done with the little money their father had left; had she made any investments; had she sold the piece of land they possessed near Nauplia; had she considered Eugenia's future; and so on. His composure was so beautiful, so civilised that in its presence Madame Nini became a different woman, shy, diffident, restrained. As for Eugenia, she never spoke a word, but kept her eyes fixed on her brother.

But Madame Nini couldn't keep it up very long. The strain was too great. Soon she began to whimper.

"I don't know why you are asking me all these questions . . . I don't understand, what is it you want?"

"It is in your own interest, my dear mother; yours and Eugenia's."

"You've been away all these years, in a fine college, meeting fine people. You don't know what I've been through. Life has been very hard. And on top of everything I have an ungrateful wretch of a daughter. What has she been telling you? She makes my life a misery. . . . What have I done to her? What have I done to you? Why do my children persecute me?"

She was comfortably in tears now. And at the sight of tears Eugenia woke up, like an animal at the smell of blood. She laughed ferociously: "Lies! See how she's trying to get out of it! Oh, how I know those tears! Look at me, look at me close, and let's see if you can go on crying!" The two women faced each other panting, two old adversaries who had used up each other's sadism in an endless game of see-saw, yet were ready to fight once more over whose turn it was to persecute.

Orestes rose, his smooth face disturbed for the first time since he had arrived. "I will not have this," he said, "will you be quiet, both of you, at once."

But they were lost to the world, perfect partners caught in their war dance round a wavering pole of power.

Orestes withdrew in himself, shrivelled up, cold with disgust. "This is disgraceful. I shall leave you till you have recovered your senses." And he left in a huff, oddly spinsterish.

They paused only for a second as the door closed behind him. Then they threw themselves back into the fight, using untried words, letting blows loose with an abandon more complete, more drunken than ever before. Perhaps they sensed this might be the last time.

When Eugenia saw Orestes again, at the hotel, she had a bruised, penitent look. She kept her eyes lowered as he remonstrated against her behaviour.

"You were utterly hysterical," he said, "both of you. A couple of hysterical fishwives. I have never seen anything so disgusting."

Eugenia cried out: "She accused me, you heard what she. . . ." Then she gave up, bowed her head again. "You are right. That is what I have become. That is what she has made of me. . . ."

"I am glad you realize it."

"It's living with her all these years. You don't know what it does to one. You don't know, you don't know. . . ."

"That is no excuse. I could hardly recognize you. How can you allow yourself to behave like that. How can you allow yourself to live like that, in that filthy house. I suppose you don't notice the dirt anymore. I suppose you're used to it!"

"No, no!" she begged.

He went on for some time. Never raising his voice, never touching her. Finally he went over to the washbasin and washed his white hands, saying: "And about those shirts. Don't bother about them, I've found a laundry near here that will take them. It will save you the trouble."

Her heavy marble face, resting on her chest, did not stir, the eyelids remained closed, but a dull red flush crept over it. Once again, the strange, angry shame gripped her, more anger than shame; her eyes burnt with the same rebellious tears.

"What could I do? I had to stay there. You've got to understand. I had to be there and wait for you. I just held on as best I could, till you came and put an end to it all, and did what I couldn't do. Now you're here," she suddenly burst out, "and what did you do? All you did was talk money!"

"I know what I am doing. I would have tackled the rest later. One has to go carefully about these things."

"Carefully?" she cried.

"Yes. One must take care to collect enough evidence before one can make an official accusation. It takes time."

"What more evidence do you want? That house! That woman! And he . . . lying in her bed, wrapped in her shawls, her 'little pasha,' her Holy Man . . . you had only to push the bedroom door . . . it was all there, all there!"

"I don't mean that," he said, annoyed. "I mean the magazine. It is a severe offence, they could be sentenced for that. If they are found guilty, they shall be sent to prison, I shall see to it. I promise you."

She looked at him aghast.

"Who cares about the magazine?" she cried. "What has prison to do with it?"

"It has everything to do with it. What, are you defending them now? What would you have me do?"

She paused, absolutely still. Then she flung at him: "Kill her!"

"Orestes! Kill her," she repeated quietly, with force.

The look of puzzled disgust came over his face again.

He shrugged. "Don't be absurd. One doesn't kill people like that—"

"No, one doesn't kill people like *that*," she said bitterly.

"But I shall turn them over to the police. It is my duty. If they are found guilty, of course."

Suddenly she asked:

"You don't hate her?"

He shrugged, frowned: "Not the way you do. No, I don't think so. Of course I think she has behaved abominably. . . ."

She cut him short brutally, she was all flashes now.

"Then leave her alone! A woman like her—you either hate her to death, or you leave her alone. You mustn't go near her again." She was ablaze with a strange, distorted loyalty.

He raised his eyebrows, nearly smiled. "Well! Then . . . what is to be done? Do you perhaps intend . . . doing it yourself after all?"

"No," she said with certainty, in a very low voice, "I can't. I am too close to her."

"So what do you suggest? After all, the magazine must. . . ."

"Go away," she said quickly. "Go away. At once. Leave us alone."

"Eugenia," he said. But something very final in her face silenced him.

"At least," he said after a while, "would you consider coming with me? Think it over. Let me know tomorrow. Things might look different to you then."

"No," said Eugenia. "I can't come. As long as she is alive, I must go on hating her. I must be near her, hating her. That is my life. Go away, you have nothing to do here."

He looked helpless, the immaculate young man in the white shirt. And it was she who would not touch him now.

When she got home she looked around her as if after a long absence. Madame Nini, sensing that her power was more secure than ever, nosed around her, full of temptations. But Eugenia, oblivious, looked out of the kitchen window, breathed in the kitchen stench, like a seaman on deck who has cut off the moorings of his ship and abandoned himself to his element, the sea with her tides and her monsters.

THE EXILE

It was a harsh cold day, mid-winter, so the boy couldn't pretend he was a tourist. Even in summer, very few tourists came here. Then the long fighting on the mainland made travelling for pleasure even more improbable. But peace-time or wartime, there had never been much to see here. The big holiday ships kept away. The harbour was extremely shallow, and the voyage was too long anyway. But obedient to his instructions, the boy wandered up and down the pier; he gazed at the houses, admired the sea-view from the jetty; he tried to look leisurely, even bored. It was difficult, for he felt excited and impatient.

At lunch-time he gave a sigh of relief, he could make his first move. He walked along the waterfront slowly to see which restaurant was most crowded, so that his presence in it would not be too conspicuous. It took him some time to find out. The restaurants were undistinguishable, at first glance, from the other shops and establishments; the windows were as dirty, difficult to see through; the walls were the same dingy colour, the signs above the entrance small, obscure, with no intention to advertise, only inform; the chairs and tables which in summer would have been under an awning outside and might have guided him, had all been moved indoors.

He finished by singling out the restaurants eventually, there were only two of them. Neither was very crowded. In a place like this people only ate in a restaurant out of necessity, having nowhere else to go; there were a few bachelors, a few widowers, several drunks. Even the strangers who had come to work here (the school-teacher, the harbour-master, the police sergeant) had brought over their wives or got themselves wives, and made a home, because it was more economical.

The boy sat down at a table in the centre, and nodded all around two or three times. He had a nice face, he was not too well-dressed, so the people at the other tables soon spoke to him. They didn't ask him at once what he was doing on the island. But there was something ruthless in their set faces, encircling him, watching, that meant they intended finding out sooner or later. He didn't make them wait. He must not appear mysterious. He said he'd come to enquire about an uncle of his who had once been a political prisoner on the island.

"We haven't heard from him for some months. We enquired at the Ministry, but they were very vague. They can't be bothered at a time like this."

"What was his name?" said one of the closed, sallow faces.

"That one!" several voices cried out when they heard the name. "That one has been dead over a year now." Some of them laughed. It was rather a joke; ignorance of any kind made them laugh. A man at a corner table explained to a drunk: "No, he had no idea—he's come all this way looking for a man who's dead!" He spoke loudly as one speaks to a deaf person.

The boy composed a sad face, not too sad, while the laughing frittered away. Then he asked:

"Are there no more political exiles left on the island?"

"There's one left. Just one. Way up in the hills."

"He's been there two years."

Their faces turned serious.

"What's his name?" asked the boy.

"We call him the Commander."

Another man put in: "Commander Rigas."

"We just call him the Commander. I don't think Rigas is his real name."

"Perhaps he can tell me some more about my uncle," said the boy. "Perhaps they lived together up in the hills."

"Perhaps. But this one keeps very much to himself."

"Doesn't he come down here to the village at all?"

"Oh, once in a while. He buys tobacco. He buys a lot of tobacco. So as not to have to come down often."

"The other one, your relative, he was here all the time. He went round the cafés, every day. . ." They laughed again, the joke was still alive.

"Perhaps it's his back—it's the Commander I'm talking about. He was wounded in the war. When they brought him here he was still very bad. Perhaps he doesn't like walking."

"No, no," one of the men said impatiently, "It's not the wound, he likes to keep to himself. He can walk all right. People have seen him climbing where even the goats won't go. He doesn't talk much either."

"He's a character," someone said in a low voice, meditatively.

"But how does he live," asked the boy, "how does he feed himself?"

"He's got a gun. He's a good shot."

"A good shot," they nodded, several of them.

"But do they allow him to carry a gun? A prisoner?" said the boy, looking surprised.

They shrugged. "It's only a small calibre. For birds. Perhaps a hare. There's not much he can do up there."

"Isn't he guarded?"

"Guarded! Why should they guard him? He can't get away; everybody knows his face, if he tried to get on the ship. There's not much he can do. That's why they chose our island for political exiles, because it's so far away from the mainland, from other islands. Besides, all these exiles, usually they don't want to get away. It's quiet here, it's cheap, they've had enough, they don't want to get mixed up in all that mess again, on the mainland. Glad they're out of it."

After a silence, someone asked: "And how's the fighting going on over there?"

"It's still going strong, up in the North," said the boy. "There are still a lot of guerillas hiding in the mountains. They say it'll take some time to clear the mountains."

The faces were dubious, sullen; indifferent at heart, but they liked to appear interested in politics, in the Situation.

"You haven't got yesterday's paper, have you?"

The boy gave them the two papers he carried in his pocket. Shuffling and whispering, a clinking of glasses; attention gradually fell away from him. Before it had quite gone, he reached out tentatively:

"Perhaps I could go and see the Commander?"

"He might be able to tell me something about my uncle," he reminded them. "Something I can tell his wife. You know."

"I suppose you could go," said the waiter who came to take his plate. "I shouldn't think the police sergeant would mind. But it's a long way off. Three or four hours' walk . . ."

"Do you think I might get lost?"

"There's only the one path."

"Well, perhaps I'll go tomorrow," said the boy.

In spite of the paraffin lamps, the cafés looked bleaker in the evening. The lights laid them bare; they were too big, they could never be filled. The marble table-tops had a dull, yellow glisten, like wet pavements in an empty street; they bore the innumerable wet circles of a day's used glasses. One of the cafés had a torn billiard table. Men drifted in, out, one could tell the day was dragging to an end, one could tell there was nothing to do afterwards. The boy walked along the pier twice. But it was cold and very dark. The dreary island evening, the lonely island winter very nearly touched him, but again and again the thought of the man in the hills revived him; and then the hours, no longer inert, rolled and leapt ahead of him, a tumble of expectations.

Along the pier one light shone brighter than the rest. The boy noticed it on the way back from the jetty, with the full black night at his back. The brightness made it look like a place of festivities and he walked to it, though he knew it could be nothing of the sort, not here. It was a barber's shop. It was small and narrow and its walls white, which accounted for the concentrated brilliance. The lamp was acetylene instead of paraffin, so that there was no yellow tinge, it was almost like electricity. There was just one barber's chair, and it was occupied. Four or five people were seated on a bench waiting their turn. The boy sat next to them. He could be shaved now instead of doing it himself painfully next morning with cold water, in the room he had rented above the restaurant.

His turn was long in coming. But the barber seemed prepared to stay open all night. People dropped in. A woman in a shawl entered, delivered a message to one of the men and disappeared again. Two or three small dirty boys hovered whispering at the door, shy and impudent at the same time. Then a young man came in laughing; after some bantering with the men he went out and returned with a guitar. He played it standing up, strolling round the shop, stooping over one man, then another, crouching at the barber's feet. He left most of his songs unfinished, he didn't know them well or had enough of them; then he'd throw back his head and start another one. Meanwhile the barber told stories with a professional air, his razor suspended.

The boy was happy, charmed. In the hum of talk and guitar, he found a companion, the dark, short man who sat beside him on the bench. This man seemed to echo his own thoughts aloud, and approached him with a curiosity equal to his own.

"So you're going up to see him tomorrow?"

"Yes."

"I wish I could come with you. But he doesn't like strangers. With you it's different, you're his relative, aren't you?"

"No, I've never set eyes on him."

"But you know him; you know about him. You know more than us. What was he before they sent him here? That's what I want to know. He was something big, wasn't he? Not just a commander. A general?"

"He was something in the war. It was before my time. Not a general, I don't think so. Didn't the police sergeant tell you why they sent him here? You should be the ones to know, not me."

"The sergeant! He doesn't know anything. He says they're all communists. He says all the political exiles that are sent here are communists."

"Does he look like a communist?"

"How should I know? As if we saw a lot of communists in this god-forsaken place. We're outside the game, we know nothing. Even when the war was on, we only knew of it because we were hungrier than usual." After a pause the man said: "Besides, I've only seen him once. . . ."

"Does he look old?"

"Not very. Middle-aged. He has iron-coloured hair, an iron-coloured moustache. He looks very proud. And worried; always frowning. . . ."

"Worried? There shouldn't be much to worry him up there in the hills. I thought he would have a calm look, very calm—"

"Who knows? Perhaps it was only an impression."

They were silent. The barber wiped his razor meticulously on the roll of toilet paper hanging at the back of the chair. The guitarist hummed absently in between two songs. Then the dark man next to the boy stooped a little and whispered haltingly: "Shall I tell you what he did once? He set fire to the forest, in the middle of the night. The sergeant said he must have been trying to make signals. He wanted to keep him in jail, or even send him back to Athens, to a proper camp. But the Commander swore it hadn't been that; he did it in a moment of madness, he said. He argued and argued with the sergeant, he's a fine talker when he feels like it. If he'd wanted to make a signal, he said, he would have lighted a small fire on the edge of the cliff, by the sea, where it's all rock, he didn't have to set fire to the whole forest, did he?" The man asked the question triumphantly, while the guitarist, as if knowing, as if in accompaniment, burst into a new song, full and passionate.

The man and the boy laughed together tasting the victory of the hero in the hills as if it were wine, warming the wine in their hands, each his own glass, his own share of it.

"Do you think, perhaps, he's gone a bit mad up there all on his own?"

"Who knows? I wouldn't be surprised. But who knows? I never see him. It makes me angry: the only thing that ever happens here, the only thing this damned place is known for, is the political exiles. And we never see them. . . ."

Something was worrying him. He frowned.

"You say you don't know him personally," he said to the boy. "But at least you've heard things, you know more than us—it is certain, isn't it, that he was something big? A great man?"

"Yes. He was a great man."

The boy came within sight of the hut in the hills towards evening. It had been a difficult journey. His uneasiness had grown as he progressed. What right had he to be here? The trees were a very dark green, tall and stern, the sky was grey. Complete silence followed him all the way, except for the knock of his boots against the rocky path. As he climbed higher the trees became sparser; there were just a few isolated ones, mutilated by the wind, and a great deal of grey rock interspersed with short, prickly bushes. The path was steeper so that now his horizon was studded with sharp profiles—tree-profiles and rock-profiles, great lonely shapes against the void of the sky. The boy longed for the sight of the hut; at the same time he did not expect any real warmth from it. It would be part of this hostile nature, it belonged to this alien world.

The hut seemed empty when he reached it; windows and door were closed. A low wall, like a fence, encircled it. The boy walked slowly round the house. At the back he found the man he was looking for. He was sitting on the wall with his legs hanging over the outer side. His back was a bit hunched, his hands clasped between his knees. He was absolutely motionless.

He did not hear the boy, who was able to walk up almost to his side; he was even able to see part of the man's face. The expression on it was completely vacant. At last the boy spoke. The man gave a great start. Then he stared at the boy in anguish.

"What are you doing here?" he cried roughly. Then, quieter: "You are not from the village. You are a stranger. You've just arrived on the ship—" an uncertain eagerness crept into his face.

The boy said: "I have been sent by Apergis."

The eagerness did not quite leave the man's face; only it became coupled to an incongruous, superimposed sarcasm as he replied: "I thought they had forgotten all about me."

"I will try to explain," said the boy falteringly.

"Explain!" he laughed. "What can you know about it? Only what they told you. Let's go into the house. It's horrible out here. Or are you impressed by the view?" He was sarcastic again. He did not wait for the boy's answer but led him to the house.

Once in the house he became feverishly active. He lit a storm-lamp, then a small rusty paraffin stove. He fetched a chair, swept a few old, hard crumbs from the table with his palm. Then he hurried to a cupboard to fetch a bottle of yellowish wine, half a loaf of bread, and white cheese that still had some goat's hair in it. Before he sat down, he went to the windows to check if they were properly shut.

He drew up a stool, looked at the boy searchingly: "All right now? Are you comfortable?"

The boy was embarrassed by the fuss. He didn't know how to take it; he had been full of humbleness and wanted to be allowed to use it.

"Please let me talk to you," he stammered. "I've been waiting for this moment—I'm not as ignorant as you think. I know what happened. I know they betrayed you."

"But it couldn't be helped, isn't that it?" the man said with a short loud laugh, a bark of a laugh.

"Perhaps it couldn't be helped, I can't tell," said the boy with vehemence. Then softly: "I also know they wouldn't have done it—they couldn't have done it—if the Chief had been still alive. The Chief loved you very much, didn't he? You were his right hand."

"Yes," said the man, with a bitter smile.

"I know," the boy said. "Still, you can't expect the same thing from the others. They are not the same type of men. They are more—practical. And then things didn't go so well. But all the same I know that Apergis respects you. I know that for sure." He swallowed hard, then tried to add nonchalantly:

"Apergis wants you back. He needs you."

The man flushed violently. He was silent, his eyes fixed. It was some time before he spoke: "What on earth would Apergis need me for?" He tried to laugh again.

He suddenly got up and went to the door. He opened it and leaned forward, his hands gripping the low lintel above his head.

The boy was left alone again and full of awe in the dark presence of this man, the dark hunched back which concealed anger and grief, anger hurled out silently into the great night outside. But he continued bravely:

"They need you, Apergis's guerilla-band is falling to pieces. The men are demoralized. They don't trust Apergis the way they trusted the Chief. He is a good leader, he is brave and very clever, but it is no longer the same. If you came back, things might change—You were the Chief's best friend. You knew all his secrets, all his thoughts." The boy hesitated a little: "And you have his memoirs, his last instructions, the ones he wrote before he was killed. Apergis believes there might be something there to give the men faith again. It is enough that they are the Chief's words. The effect on their morale may be incalculable, Apergis says."

The man suddenly swung round from the door. A secret excitement twitched in his face:

"And how do you know I still have the papers?" he asked. "When I was sent here, everything was finished. . . . The Chief, and me, and the papers, all that belonged to the past. Finished. . . . Done away with. Rubbish. And what do you do with rubbish? You throw it away."

"You destroyed the papers?" whispered the boy.

"Who knows," said the man thoughtfully, "who knows?"

The boy did not insist but watched him without speaking.

The silent hills of the daytime had found a voice now; there were owls, there was a fitful undecided wind coming through the open door. The hut creaked a little. In the room where they sat there was a continuous wheezing sound, the boy couldn't tell if it was the stove or the lamp. He grew thoughtful too. Now the lamp had them both staring at it, a small flame flickering through smoky glass.

"You hate them, don't you?" said the boy.

The man only smiled. He might have been thinking of something else.

"What is your name?" he asked the boy after a while.

"Stamos."

"And you are—eighteen?"

"Nineteen."

"I don't suppose you've actually been in the fighting."

"Not *in* the fighting. . . . But I hang around. I've lived with them in the mountains, up north. I help Apergis with his papers, I look after his clothes, his boots. Sometimes I help the cook. I carry messages. Apergis lets me carry a gun. My father was a friend of his. He is good to me."

"But you don't stay in the mountains all the time? You go down to the cities?"

"Yes, sometimes. I can go and come, I'm only a boy, so they don't think I'm dangerous," sighed the boy. "Though it is getting more difficult now."

"The cities must be almost back to normal, now that the fighting is far away."

"Yes. In Salonica, you still feel a kind of tension, like in wartime. But in Athens you can hardly tell there's anything going on. The wireless of course, bragging and mouthing big words, all that silly propaganda; but who listens to the wireless. You hear about arrests; houses are raided; there are a lot of uniforms in the streets. But it's as if it were all the State's private affair. Most people are beginning to have a good time again, to think of their own affairs. Much they care what we go through."

"Tell me more about Athens."

The tone of his voice made Stamos look up sharply; and he had time to capture on the lined face an extraordinary expression of avidity. He asked suspiciously: "You miss Athens then?"

Rigas shrugged. Finally he said: "Perhaps I fear it more than I miss it. Tell me more about Athens all the same. To pass the time."

Stamos told him about Athens. Most of the theatres were playing reviews, musicals, political satires, but the censorship was still strict. The cinemas had begun bringing American and English films. There were a lot of Americans about. For some time now there had been a big organization in Athens, with many offices, it was called UNRRA; some of his friends had found jobs there as lorry-drivers, messenger-boys even. They paid well. You could get American cigarettes quite cheaply. The autumn had been long and warm. A month ago there had still been cane chairs outside the cafés in Constitution Square. At the Old Palace, the men who guarded the Unknown Soldier were no longer evzones but members of the armed forces, they took turns, one week it was sailors, then airmen, then soldiers. The evenings were still clear, the sunsets very bright, but now you could see grey clouds racing behind the Acropolis, over the sea. The shops had turned on their luminous signs again; Omonoia square looked wonderful at night; and so crowded. . . . The whole of Athens was crowded; thousands of people streaming in from the provinces, the destroyed villages.

Rigas listened, his face quite hermetic. The boy slowly came to a stop. After a long silence, he asked: "I suppose it must be lonely up here. Why don't you go and live down in the village? You're allowed to, aren't you?"

"Yes. But I don't want to. I can't have the sergeant watching me all the time. And people are a nuisance. They ask questions, they take sides, they argue, they quarrel. You get mixed up without wanting to."

"And you're fed up with all that . . ." said the boy reverently. He walked to the open door and looked out. "It takes guts to live out here," he said.

"It's all right," said Rigas, neutrally.

"Will you show me around tomorrow? You must know the place inside out. It is your kingdom," he said shyly.

"There is not much to see. But I'll take you around."

"Do you ever sleep out of doors? When the weather's good. I love doing that."

"No, never." His voice had gone very cold. "Shut the door. We will make a bed for you."

He passed a hand across his face. "Your coming has done strange things to me," he said. "You must forgive me if I seem moody."

In one bed there was Stamos, who slept off the fatigue and the novelties of yesterday, who slept with all his body, thickly, wholly. In the other bed, Rigas, who slept badly. He groaned and tossed; the boy's presence was like a clock ticking in the room; he couldn't shut it out, it dragged him back to the slow, parcelled minutes of consciousness. Rigas could not cross over the border into freedom; the freedom of sleep, where there is no time; the blank freedom of the days before the boy's arrival. He was caught in the ticking minutes; this was time, this was the night going by, trickling away in minutes towards a dawn, a day—a day in which Stamos would awake and talk and question, in which there would be changes and shiftings, actual happenings that had repercussions, that would affect his companion, then himself, then others beyond, in ever-widening circles, in a concatenation unbroken like the ticking minutes of this time-bound night. His thoughts exhausted him; each minute a new thought, each minute fashioning its own thought; a continuous refraction in the passing stream, a dazzling, maddening light distributed into a thousand watery fragments.

Twice he lifted his head from his pillow to look at Stamos's dark form at the other end of the room. He could not get used to this being in the room, this obstacle against which all his silent words broke and came flickering back to him, instead of being lost forever, like the innumerable words he had lost before Stamos came; words lost, gone, swallowed by the watery waste which had served him as time until now.

He nearly got up from his bed to go and look at Stamos, stoop over him—a curious, passionate, fearful Psyche stooping over Eros, and in his limbs the same strange weakening that shook the hand that held the fatal taper.

And Stamos, not quite oblivious, sensed something of these strange movements and sounds from the other bed. Round his thick sleep they circled, infinitely repeated, elongated in the peculiar perspective of sleep, like a cry stretched out in a tunnel, so that he had the impression the whole night was one single groan; not his groan. As if he lived the other man's nightmare indirectly, ran parallel to it without ever being touched by it; so that he woke with a borrowed, alien anxiety nagging at his brain, an anxiety incongruous in this body of his which lay quite intact, the same familiar body he found in his bed every morning.

Rigas had already left his bed, the house was empty. Stamos discovered he was alone with disappointment, but without surprise. He had expected, known that he and Rigas could not wake together, start the day together. Rigas was the man you could not catch up with, the man whose direction could never be toward you. In his very few memories of Rigas, the memories of one evening, it was always a profile that appeared, a half-face only; a face in the process of turning away.

Stamos wanted to leave the house at once, find him. Rigas was up in the dark hills, breaking through what trees, climbing over what rocks, listening to what voices. Rigas was already conversing with this blank new day, he held the shape of it. And Stamos was alone in a house where Rigas was not. He was of no use to himself, his single existence suddenly of no value at all.

There was no sign of Rigas outside. Stamos looked round the back of the house, then down the path that led to the house. The evening before, arriving from the village, he had looked for him in the same way. All during the long march from the village to the hut his eyes had been on the look-out for him. "I am hunting down a free man," he thought, and felt sordid. But he went on searching, and even formulated a separate thought: "I must bring the conversation back to Apergis. I must make him decide."

Rigas was not very far away. He was drawing water from a well, hardly a well, a hole in the ground, down in a small ravine on the left of the hut.

Rigas and Stamos did not speak much at first; as if the long, long night with its own happenings had left them with nothing to say, had enacted all the important conversations. Stamos, in his youth, was the first to shake off the predestination, and set his face determinedly towards the day ahead. "Let's go," he pleaded.

"You'll have to wait," Rigas said gruffly. He went into the house, and after some time reappeared with a saw and axe, and a piece of bread. He was also carrying his gun.

"We are going to cut down some wood in the hills," he said. "I hate purposeless wanderings. You take the axe, I'll carry the rest."

"Do you always carry your gun?" the boy asked, slightly abashed, but happy all the same, happy they were setting out, he and Rigas.

"Always. You never know."

They started to climb the slope behind Rigas's hut. Stamos halted a minute to look up and take in the whole sky, the hills, the wilderness. Rigas, in front of him, advanced slowly, sturdily, his eyes fixed to the path, like a labourer tilling a field.

All through that day Stamos tried to see with Rigas's eyes, hear with his ears. And he thought he sensed things he had never sensed before. This landscape was not the green, sylvan nature of mythology and fairy-stories; nor was it the blue and white nature of postcard Greece. This landscape was almost northern in its ruggedness. He tried to remember the mountains up north with Apergis and the guerillas; there had been many more trees, taller and fuller ones. But that had not been nature; it had been "headquarters," "centre of operations," "our side of the slope," "a good vantage-point."

The ground had never been so hard, harsh, grainy under his feet. His ankles knocked against stones like wood against wood, the low thyme-shrubs scraped against the rock like metal instruments. Even the few gaunt trees seemed to scrape the sky. The muted tints, clear grey rock, green-black foliage, patchy brown earth, dry purple thyme and heather, were as violent in their clearness as the most fiery of colours. The smells, frozen and concentrated by the winter, were as strong as ether. And the whole air was occupied by a vast unexpressed booming, which was the voice of silence, but not of solitude; not even solitude, it was too inhuman for that; solitude is a man separated from his surroundings; this place would allow no separation, it was all there was.

Stamos looked at Rigas as if he had been the revelation itself, not simply the revelator; as if the great absent booming has issued from his frame. Yet Rigas had pointed out nothing, made no comments. He had limited himself strictly to practical information, technical details. He showed the boy where the wild rabbits had their burrows. He examined the weather. He chose passages through the rocks. He picked a few herbs. When they began to cut down the wood, he knew at a touch whether a tree was sound or rotten inside. Rigas's knowledge impressed Stamos more than the unveiling of loftier mysteries. These were the certain signs of the initiate, they indicated a sure casual mastery, a communication with nature that was made not of words and emotions, but acts.

"Are you cold?" Rigas asked Stamos, noticing that the boy was blowing on his fingers. "The winter is hard here."

"Can you see the village from up here?" the boy asked.

"No, the village is hidden away, from wherever you stand."

"One might even forget it is there," said the boy, bemused.

"Yes."

"Is this the part of the forest you set fire to?"

"So they told you about that too!" He was amused; or only contemptuously amused. "They must have told you a whole lot of nonsense about it. I can imagine."

"They did talk about it quite a lot," the boy nodded, "it has become a kind of legend in the village."

Rigas's face turned ferocious. "It was an accident," he said.

Towards noon he took Stamos to a small, shallow cave in the rock; before entering it, he knocked and prodded at the creviced walls with the muzzle of his gun. "You never know," he said mechanically. "We may not be the only ones who thought this would make a good shelter." They sat down and ate bread and rested.

Rigas looked from his boots to his gun to his piece of bread. Stamos looked outward, the narrow aperture from which he looked making the landscape open out away from him in an even wider sweep. The rocky slope falling away below him had the power of one continuous, suspended avalanche.

"I've never seen a place like this," said the boy in a low voice. "A place fit for eagles."

"I haven't seen any eagles around here," Rigas said smiling. "Only crows. They make an ugly sound, I don't like them. Perhaps I'm afraid of them. If I get killed up here—a fall, an accident, it's easy—they're the ones who will get me, and no one will know."

"You've forgotten," said the boy, "you're supposed to be coming back with me. So the crows will never get you. Or perhaps you haven't forgotten. Perhaps you've decided to stay. Is that what I must tell Apergis?"

"Apergis, ah, yes," sighed Rigas. He lifted his head and looked outward for the first time, like the boy.

Stamos didn't wait for anything more, he trod on Rigas's vagueness with perfect assurance. "From the moment I met you I knew there wasn't much hope of your coming," said Stamos. "Even before I met you, perhaps I knew."

"What was the use of coming here then?"

"Apergis sent me. He should have known better. I could never have persuaded you. Because if I'd been you, I'd have done the same. I'd have stayed. At least, I hope so. I don't know—I'm younger than you, weaker. Perhaps I'd have been tempted a bit at first."

Stamos glanced at Rigas sideways. Rigas was silent, he was chewing bread, listening or not listening, but certainly not judging. The cave, and the stony landscape outside, the mountain, were as silent; enormous, powerful, yet not overwhelming, not interested in overwhelming. Stamos felt a great freedom.

"There is something about those cities," Stamos said. "Athens, Piraeus, Salonica. Athens . . . I know Athens better. I like the noise. Up in the mountains I couldn't sleep the first nights because there was no noise. I like the smell of petrol from the cars on the thoroughfares. I can't see why, it's a dirty smell. The pollution of the cities, they say. But I like it, every time I come back from the mountains I like it better. And the people. That's the big problem. One gets tied to them—not just the ones you love. One can't do without them, I can't do without them. . . . Even in the house, I like having my mother, my sisters calling—I don't talk to them much, they bore me, but I like them being around. And then I go out! It's an adventure every time. I'm on the look-out. . . . People, people. I think it's because . . ." he blushed, he was confessing, he was saying everything, "it's because I like showing off. You have to have people to show off to. I like talking, that's showing off. Even listening is showing off sometimes. Walking, moving your hand, turning your head, smiling, when you come to think of it almost everything you do is showing off. Doing well, making a success; even making a success of small things, like jumping off the bus neatly, fixing a plug, all that is showing off; all that you do for the others. You can't do it just for yourself. It wouldn't make sense. But for the others it does. You're showing them something; who you are, what you are. And once they know, you know too; you understand yourself, you see yourself, you are there. It is a wonderful feeling. I don't know why it is so wonderful. Whenever I feel happy I know that's what's behind it, I can tell at once, there's nothing as good, as warm. And so there's always something to look forward to, because there's always someone new to show off to; or a new way of showing off to the same person. Something is always happening. You are carried on, life is on the move."

Rigas had finished his bread. He was listening now, very still, concentrated. He wasn't even looking at the rapturous boy, only listening. But Stamos faltered. He remembered where he was. He looked at Rigas and sighed.

"That's all very well," he said in a small voice. "But would you call that a life? It's wrong, it's stupid. You show off—it means you feed on others. Like those crows. You're a parasite." He cried: "What sort of a man are you if you need others to tell you you're a man? Some things you've got to know for yourself. And that's not all, you've got to know it all the time, when you're alone on the top of a mountain or walking down University Street with a crowd. You've got to know it even when somebody new comes into the room, even when you hear new things being said and you want to say them too. Once I said something like this to some friends of mine, and they laughed, they said: you ought to be a monk."

He gave a little tentative laugh, but cut it short very quickly, not hoping for a moment that he could draw Rigas, so sombre, so still, into any kind of complicity.

"That's stupid," he went on, "it's not only monks who like to be alone, besides it's easy for those who believe in God, they're not really alone. I'm thinking of the others, the philosophers, the poets, the kings. They found out things by thinking hard. By looking inside, not by listening to other people. I've never looked inside me," he cried in distress. "I don't even know what's there. I've never been alone, just me and nothing else. All right, I've been alone in my room at night, waiting for the morning, for someone to come in—getting ready for that. I've been alone on the mountain in the tent, waiting for the boys to come back, preparing all sorts of questions. But I mean alone, as alone as can be. Without waiting for the next move. How alone can one be? What happens? You cut off everything, the luxuries, the growths, the unnecessary things, the borrowed things; you cut it all off, and what is left? That's what I want to know. That's what I want to lay my hands on. The thing that is left. It must be a great and precious thing; a tiny great precious thing, like a tiny stone. It must be the truth. If that isn't the truth—"

Rigas had closed his eyes.

"So perhaps I wouldn't be tempted after all," Stamos said softly. He clasped his hands: "Can you imagine—can it be possible not to be tempted by anything? Not to envy anything, not to fear anything?"

He looked around at the empty landscape, he breathed deeply. "No interference. To move your hand like this, to say this or the other thing, because you want it, mean it, no other reason. To do only what is necessary. To look at the next day and ask nothing. To sit still, without this waiting, this looking forward. I'm tired of waiting for something more, something better. I want to be where there is nothing more. I want to get there. What are we doing, playing hide-and-seek? Comparing, postponing, changing your mind. I say something and then I think: 'No, that wasn't quite right.' I buy something and I say: 'It could have been better.' I meet a man and I think 'Now I want to meet his friend.' I earn some money and I think 'What would it be like if I had the double?' I love a girl and I think 'What would it be like if she were another?' and I have no rest and I am always hungry and always waiting."

He looked at Rigas and added gently: "You don't want to go back to all that. You'll only get torn to bits again. All broken up, here and there, little bits of you in every house, every street. One bit of you living today, another tomorrow. You've forgotten all that, haven't you. You've forgotten what it's like."

"I haven't forgotten," said Rigas.

The boy was taken aback. Rigas was quite close, the nearness of his voice startled him, their boots were touching.

"I've been talking for myself," said Stamos. "Take no notice. You know best. You know it all."

But he couldn't leave Rigas alone. He still wanted to question, probe, explore. He turned in circles, uncertain yet ruthless. He had to make everything clear. Rigas was his dream, he must possess his dream.

"How did you feel when they took you away?"

"What did you expect me to feel? I felt terrible."

"Yes, but did you want to go away?"

"Oh, I was fed up," said Rigas.

"Yes," said Stamos, "of course. You must have been pretty disgusted at them all. I suppose disgust is not a bad thing. It protects you. You needn't be afraid even of remembering. Disgust takes care of that; it keeps all the memories far away, unimportant."

"And yet," he dreamed, "I would have thought one did forget. Completely. Just yourself and this place, nothing else. All the rest faded out. No interference."

Rigas smiled. "Don't worry. Sometimes one can't remember even if one tries." But his eyes were very serious, in spite of the smile.

"You'll see, you'll see," Stamos said, his excitement returning, "soon you won't remember at all; it will all go, and leave you alone, free. It's too early still, only two years."

"Only two years," said Rigas.

"You'll see, perhaps if I come back here in another two years, you won't even be able to speak to me. You'll have forgotten the language, you'll have another language."

"I'll have turned into a wild beast," said Rigas, and Stamos laughed.

"Even now you don't say much. It's me that does all the talking. But don't worry. You don't have to listen to me. Take no notice. I know you're not really taking any notice." He piled up the distance between them recklessly, lavishly.

There was all the space in the world, the space of the sky, in which to look up, in which to fling up his admiration, a stone in the vastness of the sky.

"You must only listen to one thing," said Stamos. "You must listen when I say that I understand. I will explain to Apergis. I know what to say, I understand."

Rigas lowered his eyes. He hesitated: "You haven't thought that it's perhaps necessary I should go back to them. Since they need me. Perhaps that's more necessary than the rest."

Stamos didn't answer. Even his silence was not an answer. Rigas's word had simply slipped over him. He still looked outwards, smiling. Rigas glanced at him curiously: "You're eighteen, you've lived in the mountains with brave men, you've helped them, yet you have no loyalty. You're not interested in their fighting. Don't you care what happens over there? Don't you think they're doing something worthwhile?"

Stamos was untouched by the accusation. "Yes," he said easily, "yes. I like the boys, I admire Apergis. What they are doing is brave. But this," he said almost slyly, "this is better. This is the thing."

He went on impatiently: "All right, they may be fighting for something worthwhile, but who thinks of that, who remembers! In the meantime they get mixed up in all kinds of messes. Look at what they did to you! It's like I told you; when you are with people you change all the time, you live by the day and by the moment, changing, wanting something else, something more. You can't stick to one thing. Look at Apergis. He was the Chief's friend, your friend. Then he betrayed you. Then he became chief; he became gentle, sensible, a different man. When you come, if you come, he will be your friend once more. Then perhaps you'll want to be chief. Or he will think so. He will make you think so, and then hate you for it. Can you see any sense in it all? And what about you? You will hate him. The men around you will shift from you to Apergis, from Apergis to you, helping you or lying to you. And with each man you will be a different person. You will be afraid, you will defend yourself, you will try to win over the men. Or you will be sorry, and you will be betrayed again. And so it goes on. A big racket, a big mess. If you think one has time to think of the fighting and what will happen after the fighting. One can't see clearly, it's too far, and all this changing, changing in between."

"If they need me," insisted Rigas with a great intensity.

"I don't know," muttered Stamos leaning back. "Perhaps you'd be safe anywhere. Even with them. After having lived here."

"I wouldn't want to show off," said Rigas, smiling as he used the boy's words. Then turning austere, impersonal: "That's not what I want."

Stamos cried: "So you still want something?" Innocent and inquisitorial, he was like a child-priest, a child-king, whom one can obey more blindly than a grown, knowing man.

"Perhaps I only want to serve," said Rigas.

The boy shook his head contemptuously. "You've gone beyond all that."

Rigas recoiled a little at the contempt, although it was not directed at him. Then he remembered who Stamos was talking to. He looked out of the cave again, far out, the tautness went from his face. He seemed to let go of something. He shrugged: "To hell," he said, "what business have I over there? What business have I with Apergis? You've made me dizzy with all your talking. I'm not used to it, I'd rather cut wood all day. We're going back now, it will be dark soon. And I'm tired."

Yet he got up with a strange alacrity. For a second he looked down at Stamos searchingly, as if to confirm something. Having found what he wanted, he picked up two bundles of wood and swung them on to his shoulder; then glanced at the great slope spreading away, and the dark trees gathered below; and he raced towards them as if to meet something found again, or something newly discovered. He didn't wait for Stamos, didn't look back once, knowing that he was followed, and watched.

It was dark very quickly. Rigas broke into a song, his voice raucous and mocking. It was a soldier's song, the words were coarse and gay. The race down the slope seemed to have intoxicated him. The owls began tooting, and Rigas answered them, with great bursts of laughter. Once or twice he disappeared into the trees; when he emerged he did not explain what he had been up to. Stamos didn't ask him. Now he was completely safe in his admiration. The change in Rigas did not surprise him. Perhaps he did not even notice it, for this was the image of Rigas he had been carrying in his thoughts all along, he had seen no other. The idol was becoming itself, making itself visible.

Stamos stayed another day. He admitted it was not necessary; the decision had been made, he had his message ready for Apergis. The matter had been settled yesterday, on the hill-top. He sensed there had been a conflict, though he had been almost the only one to speak and there had been no argument. Then Rigas had freed himself, had left it all behind him as he raced down the slope, declaring himself at last, taking open possession of his territory. And Stamos could not speak anymore, after having spoken so much. He had nothing to say; he was empty and happy. His dream was completed, his dream had grown real; he felt wonderfully unnecessary.

Only Rigas existed, who after having been so tentative, so veiled, seemed guided now by an extraordinary assurance. "He has come to himself," Stamos thought, "he's recovered from my intrusion, he is himself again."

Rigas came and went, leapt to his feet, lay down on the ground, with clean-cut suddenness, obeying himself without question. His hidden power, released, branched out in all directions, a constant assertion. He neglected Stamos, left him alone, often ignored him completely. All day long, he sang the coarse mocking soldier's song. From the hut, Stamos heard snatches of it echoing through the trees, and felt the whole mountain was inhabited and he was listening to forbidden music. Towards evening he couldn't hear Rigas's song anymore, only the rippling shots from his gun. Several times the rocks clapped back their ghostly applause. Then a long time passed during which he heard neither song nor gunshots. He waited, perfectly patient.

Rigas came back at night, carrying a hare and two turtle-doves. He threw them on the table, and sat down with his legs stretched out. He appeared glad to see Stamos. "We'll eat these tomorrow," he said. "Sometimes when I'm alone I can't be bothered. I forget about them, and they rot."

Stamos said: “I must leave tomorrow. I must leave early, the ship sails at four.”

Rigas was silent. Stamos wondered if he had heard.

Then Rigas waved Stamos away with a heavy hand and fell headlong on his bed like a stone. He went to sleep almost at once.

On his last morning, Stamos hoped to be the first up for a change. To see Rigas asleep, the mountain asleep, to get some hold, some knowledge of the place before he left. Even the most sordid of eavesdroppers is better than a spectator, he sees what is forbidden, not what is offered. During these last hours, something like ambition stirred in him, rising above his usual humility, though impregnated with it; for it was only a humble ambition after all, quickly gone. He knew he must go without leaving a mark.

Rigas's bed was empty as usual. There was a great glittering day outside, immense because of the clarity of the air, which revealed everything, in a complete, crushing statement. The sun had the perfection of winter sunshine; hard, frozen, still, flawless, as if protected by an enormous sheet of glass. The ink black shadows made the rocks look sharper, more cruel. In the distance, the sea, no longer misty, barred the horizon with a definite, violent blue.

Stamos edged his way out into the glass-encased landscape and went, resigned, towards the ravine in search of Rigas. He was washing his feet at the well, stripped to the waist. His body was white; so white and clean-cut as it stood out against the dark bushes of the ravine that it had nothing fleshly about it; it belonged to a cold, hard, mineral world. He cleaned his feet meticulously; ugly feet deformed by heavy boots, ugly useful feet. He said to Stamos:

"Get ready quickly. We should be on our way already." He jerked his head upwards to the sun, which already seemed vertical in its brightness. "He wants me out of the way," thought Stamos. He was sad, but not bitter. He obeyed, he hurried. From the first moment the hut on the mountain had been unattainable; he had never tried to be Rigas, the distance had never lessened.

"I'll go and heat some milk," said Rigas. "Something hot in the stomach for the long walk."

"Yes," said Stamos.

But Rigas changed his mind. "All right, I might as well wait for you," he said.

"What a day," said Stamos. "The place looks even more beautiful like this."

"You'll have a good trip," said Rigas. He looked at the sea.

Stamos thought of the ship, the people on the ship, the people on the quay at Piraeus. He felt he'd been away a long time. "Back again soon," he thought. And he didn't really mind, his heart even leapt a little, forward to the sea, the arrival. Immediately afterwards he felt vaguely guilty, the same feeling he had when he left his mother sitting vacantly by the window watching the evening while he went out into the lighted city. He resented his own involuntary comparison. "It doesn't apply in the least," he thought. "This time I am leaving what is best. Yet I don't mind. All I really think of is having a good time."

He followed Rigas with bent head. "I'm no good, I'll never be any good," he said. He felt cheap and comfortable, underneath his sadness.

Until the moment they left Rigas did not go off on his own like the day before. He stayed with Stamos the whole time, watchful and silent. He had the brooding face of their first evening together, except that now there was a hard line in his jaw.

"Let's go," said Rigas. "I'll walk down the path with you a bit."

He led the way as usual. The sun was full in their faces, small white stones rolled beneath their feet.

"What a day," repeated Stamos. "Will you go out shooting?"

"Perhaps," said Rigas. He shot forward, letting his body go, carried by the downhill path, by a sudden exuberance, an impatience; nothing could possibly check his flight. And where was he fleeing like this? Stamos hurried behind him. But Rigas did stop; he leapt on to a rock on the edge of the path, pulling up with a jerk. He turned round slowly and faced the mountain, his back to the sea, his shoulders squared.

"Yes, it is a good day for shooting," he said. He had quickly mastered the interrupted movement, the flight, the unknown urge; he was ready, he was making an end. "I will leave you here," he said to Stamos, who was not ready. "You know the way. Follow the path."

He stooped to Stamos from his rock, his hand outstretched. "Give my regards to Apergis," he said with his strange grimacing smile, his irony.

Stamos, in a turmoil, a last brief storm of confused feelings before becoming an ordinary person going down to meet a ship, said very quickly:

"I will. Thank you for everything. Forgive me for staying so long."

"No, not at all. I would have liked you to stay much longer."

Stamos turned away and raced down the path, wanting to cry in a sudden rage: "I don't believe you." Yet when he reached the first bend in the path his rage dropped away and he couldn't help looking back. Rigas hadn't moved from the rock. His face was no longer clear. He was a figure of stone, a faceless statue merged to the rock.

Rigas stood on the rock for a long time. He did not dare move. The outspread landscape in its glass sheath, the man in his mould of stone, they were timeless, and yet a cloud passed, a wild rabbit scurried through a bush, and it was enough to break it up.

Rigas cracked from top to toe. He stared down the path wildly, not knowing if the boy had been there an hour or a minute ago. He screamed: "Come back, damn you!"

His crazed voice kept shooting upward into the light, empty air; it got lost at once, it spread everywhere and reached nothing. He flung himself face down on the rock and sobbed. "Take me with you, for heaven's sake take me with you."

He clung shuddering to the rock until he heard the ship's siren. Then he scrambled back to the hut, a blind crumpled animal, and shut himself in.

•

Stamos did not leave at four o'clock. The ship had brought Apergis from the mainland. Stamos was numb as he greeted him, he was indifferent, as if his story were over; this had the taste of an epilogue. Of course he had to ask Apergis why he had come; his curiosity was logical and detached.

Apergis cut him short with a question of his own:

"Well, where is Rigas?"

"He won't come," said Stamos quickly, lightly, very near to insolence, as if it were his own refusal.

"I thought so," said Apergis. "That's why I've come. When you didn't return at once, I imagined something must have gone wrong. I thought you needed some reinforcement."

"Nothing's gone wrong. He won't come, that's all. He's not interested." Stamos was not interested. There were no problems, no necessities. Apergis was slightly ridiculous; his strong active body, ready to start, his tired excited travellers face, his thick traveller's clothes put on like a disguise, a uniform. His eyes were quick, full of thoughts and plans. He came from the crowded ship, he came from the tents on the mountain, from the city, where he had made contacts; the touch of human hands was all over him. He smelt like a dormitory.

"Many people were sick on the boat, it was a bad crossing," said Apergis, laughing away his disgust.

"Now then," he said when they were clear of the passenger crowd, "How far off does our friend live? Can we get there before dark? I don't want to be seen by too many people. It's a bit risky, my coming here."

"It's four hours to the hut. I've only just come down from there, I'm tired," said Stamos. The idea of going back to the hut revolted him.

"Come now! A boy of your age."

"Anyway there's no fear about your being seen. They're very curious here, but not suspicious. The police sergeant isn't around, he must be having his siesta. Besides you're not that famous."

"All right. Let's have some coffee first."

Apergis enjoyed his coffee, and the cigarette he smoked with it. He looked round at the people in the café with a tireless appetite in his eyes. Stamos's news had not disturbed him in the least.

"Well, what else does our friend say?" he asked Stamos.

"He's nobody's friend. That's what you don't understand."

"Oh, Rigas and I will always be friends, even though he doesn't know it."

He dropped the jaunty tone and looked at Stamos in the eyes: "Let me tell you something: Rigas can't do without friends."

Stamos cried proudly: "You don't know him."

"I know him better than you. We've spent the best years of our life together. Rigas," he mused with a silent laugh, "I know him like the inside of my pocket."

Suddenly Stamos wanted to get up and go back to the hut, with Apergis, at once. His reluctance was gone. He no longer wanted to keep his dream to himself. He must show it, prove it, communicate it, the whole world must know.

The time for transactions was back; Apergis's claim must be answered, and bettered.

Apergis was examining the boy shrewdly. "I wonder what he told you," he said. "He must have done a lot of talking, to get all these ideas into your head."

Stamos jumped eagerly at this triumph, which trapped him. "That's where you are wrong," he said. "Rigas hardly spoke at all."

"Then how do you know? How do you know so much about him?"

Stamos had to make a detour, offer some other merchandise. "Besides," he threw in carelessly, "those papers you're so keen on, the Chief's memoirs: he's destroyed them."

Apergis's eyes grew steely, the mouth lost its manly charm; all that humane curiosity, that interest in the world abroad was put aside. Now was business.

"All right, let's go," he said putting down his cup with a sharp click.

"Why don't you leave him alone?" cried Stamos. "Why don't you leave us alone?"

"You needn't come if you don't want to," Apergis said. He was calling the waiter, to ask for the bill, to ask for information. He knew his way around.

A panic despair came over Stamos. The drama was about to start now, up on those hills, without him. The drama was to come; it had not been beautifully completed, as he had thought. Nothing had happened. The curtain had not even risen. He had suffered, raved, applauded, and the curtain hadn't even risen yet.

"I'm coming," he whispered, and followed Apergis.

•

The hut was in darkness, the door and windows sealed.

"He must be out," said Stamos.

"At this time of the night? For God's sake, doing what?"

"He often goes out like that, at any time of the day or night. He is free to come and go, after all." Obstinately he answered in whispers, ignoring Apergis's loud voice.

"Yes, but doing what? He can't go shooting in the dark or gathering wood—what then?"

"I don't know," said Stamos, glorying in his ignorance, unfolding it like a treasure.

"Well, I'll go and find out," Apergis said simply. As he moved away he added: "He was never much of an outdoor man. But a man can change in two years. You stay here in case he comes back from another path."

Stamos cried after him: "It's dark, you'll get lost. This place is big and wild, you have to know it well."

He added: "Only Rigas knows all the by-paths," more as reassurance to himself than warning to Apergis. Rigas must not be found. He must arrive around midnight, down from the mountain top and the trees, and find them sitting on his doorstep, cold and sleepy, hungry and patient, seeking audience.

He saw Apergis was using a flashlight. Apergis was always well-equipped, he had the necessary things for every occasion. Stamos watched the wavering light, anxiously, contemptuously. "Worse than a policeman," he thought. To cover his anxiety, which was the stronger, he gloried again: "Rigas doesn't need a flashlight. Never uses one."

The night was as still as the day had been. The stillness built up an enormous, smooth high sky, steep as a cliff. There were very few owls this time. Over the skyline the gathered trees emerged like a herd of wild dark beasts, bisons, elephants in waiting. The hut did not interrupt the wilderness; it was simply another rock, on the side of the night, not on men's side. Yet Stamos moved closer to it. He felt fear, which he quickly turned into awe. He climbed the doorstep, and gently tried the door. It gave.

By the light of a match he saw Rigas lying on his bed, his eyes wide open. His face showed no surprise. He did not even look at Stamos.

"You've come back. You've come back for me," he said, like a very sick man.

Stamos lit the storm-lamp. He sat on the edge of the bed, cautiously. Rigas got hold of his hand and gripped it hard. The boy couldn't utter a word. And Rigas only smiled, shamelessly, beatifically.

Stamos burst out desperately: "I must go and call him, he's out there looking for you, I won't be long—"

"Don't leave me," said Rigas.

But Apergis was already on the doorstep. He had seen the light of the storm-lamp through the door which Stamos had left open.

"So here he is," said Apergis.

Stamos said very quickly, as if Rigas had not spoken, had not gripped his hand, as if this were a clean start, this, now: "Rigas, Apergis has come to take you away by force."

Ignoring him, Apergis came and stood over the bed. "Well, Rigas." He smiled broadly, he touched Rigas's knee. "Well, well, old friend."

Rigas stared back at him.

"You're not ill, are you?"

Rigas came back to the narrowing world, to the hut, to this room in the hut. There was Stamos by the table, in an attitude of suspense, hanging on his lips. And there was Apergis, facing him. He did not know whom to satisfy. He did not know whom to fear most.

"I fell asleep," he said slowly. "Once the sun's gone, I haven't much notion of the time."

"I have," said Apergis. "My stomach has. I am hungry. Can you feed us?"

"There isn't much in the house," said Rigas, and he got up from his bed with an effort.

"The birds," said Stamos. "The turtle-doves. What about those?"

"That's right," decided Apergis. "Stamos, you will prepare us a good meal. Rigas and I have things to talk over."

They sat at the table, the lamp between them. Apergis began giving Rigas a detailed description of the situation on the mainland; information about the men, accounts of their activities. He gave Rigas the news in a good-hearted manner, doing him a favour, a service, taking his interest for granted. And so in spite of Rigas's total silence, the two men seated at the table with the lamp between them composed a picture of intimacy. Such relations, such moments in a relationship are exclusive, and Stamos felt excluded. He clung to Rigas's silence, watched it, guarded it, insisted on it so as to neutralize the illusion of that intimacy. But the impression remained. Two old friends reunited, brothers at arms, talking about the past and already sharing a future.

Stamos opened the door and looked out into the night, restless, trying to say something. He was opening the door of Rigas's cage, he was showing Rigas his own true royal way, out there, in the night. But Rigas had his back turned to the door, and Apergis said carelessly: "Close that door, there's a draught."

When the food was ready, Stamos brought the dishes to the table and inserted himself between them with great deliberation, like a sword, like a silent judge. Apergis did not mind the intrusion, he drew Stamos into their circle easily and without second thought. He did not feel menaced; his generosity was a mark of his assurance.

Rigas had still not uttered a word. He sat hunched and stolid, like a man in somebody else's house; not opposing Apergis's invasion, but detaching himself from it. Only when he raised his glass of wine, ceremoniously, in Apergis's direction, did he make a mechanical attempt to play host. It was only a gesture, he still said nothing. Apergis took over. Raising his own glass, he said: "What shall we drink to?" He looked at Rigas steadily: "Shall we drink to your return?" he asked, very clearly, without a trace of persuasion in his voice; a straightforward question.

Rigas could not move, or speak.

Stamos watched, fascinated. Apergis could shift from courtesy, cordiality, to utter ruthlessness; from bantering to dead seriousness, and with such mastery that he managed never to give the impression of wile, diplomacy. His manoeuvres never appeared sordid. They were not manoeuvres, they were perfect, clear-cut, well-balanced moves. Even when he had betrayed Rigas, his face must have been stamped with this same unquestionable honesty. He was infallible. How was one to face him? With what was one to face him? What greater, darker faith could stand up to his daylight? Stamos, powerless, disarmed, looked toward Rigas, who was still all shadow, all mystery. He quickly drowned his own small, anticipated defeat in the shadow that was Rigas, in the mystery that could hold all possibilities. He waited.

Apergis also waited; not for very long. He put down his glass and asked, simply: "No?"

Rigas fixed his eyes not on Apergis, but on Stamos. "No," he replied to Apergis. But he seemed to speak in a dream.

Apergis tapped his fingers on the table thoughtfully. There was no anger or disappointment on his face; but the smiling courtesy had gone completely, so that there was a frightening bareness in his attitude. He was naked purpose.

He turned to Rigas: "Well, since it's like that, at least you must let me have the Chief's papers."

As Rigas didn't answer, he asked patiently: "Stamos says you have destroyed them. Have you?"

There was another pause.

"If you have destroyed them, you'd better tell me, we needn't sit here wasting our time."

"Wasting *your* time, you mean," said Rigas, roused at last.

"Yes, mine, since you have no notion of it."

He meant what he said. He was already calculating, planning, thinking whether it would be safe to go back to the village at this time of the night, catch the early ship. . . .

Rigas cried, too quickly: "I haven't destroyed the papers." Then fiercely: "But I won't part with them."

"I see," said Apergis. "Then you'll just have to come along with the papers."

"You can't make me come," sneered Rigas. Pride was an effort to him, something slow and tortuous and unnatural. But he kept it up, stubbornly. "You can beg as much as you like," he went on. "I don't need you any longer. Things have changed. You may need me, I thank you greatly for your interest, but I don't need you any longer."

Apergis's face lit up with a cool gaiety. "Rigas, let's get things clear. It's not you we need, it's the papers. We don't need you, yourself as such, any more now than we used to need you when you had the Chief's ear. Then as now, you were an intermediary, a carrier. Nothing else."

"Yet I was the one he chose," cried Rigas.

"Because you listened so well. You had the gift of devotion, which was more than I could give him," said Apergis laughing softly to himself. He straightened his face almost at once; he was never private for long. He turned back to Rigas with the same smiling interest: "Rigas, have you got it clear now?"

Rigas gripped the table; pride no longer had anything to do with the naked desperate claim that choked him. "What you say is not true," he said, holding back his breath, holding back his panic, his ruin, "he chose me because he could trust me; because I was loyal; because I lent myself to none of your conspiracies."

"You were afraid to," said Apergis, almost with compassion. "How could you venture out, with us, after such a glorious shelter?"

Rigas closed his eyes. Apergis went on, casually but very softly: "You saw it yourself. When the Chief was killed, when the shelter was gone, you became a thing once more, an object. That's why it was so easy to betray you. Among all of us, you were the easiest, the least costly to betray, because you didn't count. My poor Rigas, even the police must have thought the same. They did not bother to shoot you. They sent you here, like the silly little dissenting members of parliament of the old days."

At the other end of the table, Stamos sat petrified. He had eyes for Rigas only. He kept postponing, with a frightful intensity within himself, the catastrophe that had already happened. He was caught in an absurd race for time, the revelation of the hero would come before the catastrophe, the revelation would come at the eleventh hour. At the point of extreme tension the truth would be irresistibly ejected. Until then he must believe nothing.

And indeed, tracked, trapped, strangulated, Rigas seemed about to give out his great justifying cry. But all he did was hurl himself in a by-way.

"The fact remains," he panted, "the fact remains that I have the papers and you can't have the papers without me."

Apergis, from the depths of his perfect wholeness, gazed at him in mild wonder. "I can understand your accepting to hide in the shadow of a man like the Chief. But to hide behind a bundle of papers!"

Rigas bowed his head. "They are all I have, you said so yourself," he whispered. His struggle was over.

Stamos saw the body slackening, the voice dying out and surged forward to pick up the tension, the passion like a fallen flag. He called urgently: "Rigas, Rigas, wake up, Rigas, answer him. You don't know what you're saying. You haven't heard properly. You must tell him. You mustn't say lies, he will believe them. What do you care about the papers? You've got this place, it belongs to you, you're its master; you go out at night in the mountain, you are among the trees, on the rocks, everywhere. The sky holds you up, you speak without words. You know what none of us knows, Rigas, tell him, tell him that when you stand on a rock you are no longer a man, I saw you, I saw you myself, standing on that rock, good God, nothing dared move while you were there! Rigas, throw away the papers, give him the papers and tell him to go!"

He was drunk. He didn't need to look at Rigas any longer. He wasn't even appealing to Rigas, though his words were appealing. He was simply obeying his deepest preference; he was telling a truth he had dreamed of; selfish and childish he made himself a Rigas of his own to fit his need, still young enough, hermaphrodite enough to incarnate for a moment his own dream, becoming dream and dreamer. In the small wooden room, at the side of the two older men already acquainted with destruction, he was very much alone and absurd. Apergis looked on this absurdity quite tenderly, only just seriously enough. But on Rigas the effect was violent. Listening with face averted in weary exasperation, following step by step the operation Stamos was performing upon him, his eyes slowly turned round to the boy, and fixed themselves there in a terrible hardening of hatred. The boy raved on, he felt nothing. Then Rigas pounced and gripped him brutally by the shoulder. He opened the door, pushed Stamos toward it. "There's your night," he shouted, "your big wonderful night. There's your mountain, your trees, your rocks. All yours! Go out in it then, go out and tell me what you've seen, what you've heard! Go out then! You had me once, with your big words. You filled me with words till I was dizzy. Then you left, carefree as a bird, off to your ship, like a damned inspector after his round, you left and there was nothing, nothing, the words were all gone, as good as the wind. That is what was left. That is what is always left. You wanted to know, didn't you? Then go out and find out! Go!"

He shook him, he held him half-bent over the threshold, as over a window with the void below. Then he let him go abruptly. Stamos remained where he was, a flung thing against the open door. He didn't move or speak.

"Why don't you go?" raged Rigas. "Go on, it's all there! It's waiting for you! There!" He pointed at the dark frenziedly.

Stamos closed his eyes tightly and whispered: "There's no place for me out there."

"No place? There's plenty of place! All the place in the world!" He checked himself, moved swiftly forward and gripping Stamos by the hand dragged him outside.

"I'll take you out," he said in a low hurried voice. "I'll show you. I'll show you the works! Everything. I am doing the honours!"

When they had gone a small distance from the house and the darkness settled in a circle around them, he let go of Stamos's hand, and the boy, lost, was aware of nothing but a ferocious laughter bobbing madly around him, up and down, now close by, now farther away.

"Rigas," he called, "don't go, I don't know where I am."

Behind him he could only just see the hut, the narrow light coming through the open door, and the black figure of Apergis, leaning idly against the doorpost. The lineaments were quite clear, yet the distance seemed infinite, because Apergis, the hut could not be reached; the way onlookers on a quay, no matter how close, seem minute and lost forever to the person on the deck of a ship that is sailing away.

Stamos cried out again: "I can't move, come back."

"I'm here," said Rigas, quite near. "Don't be afraid. I was afraid too, the first months. Not like you, much worse. Because I am the kind of man who is always afraid. Apergis told you so and you must believe him."

"I am only afraid of the dark, really," Stamos said unsteadily.

"I was afraid of the dark, I was afraid of the daylight, I was afraid of the sun at its brightest. I was alone. I had never been alone before. There had always been the Chief, Apergis told you; or someone like the chief. I was soft and naked as a worm flung out of his dark hole."

His voice moved away. A tree seemed to stand between them, or his back was turned to Stamos, because the sound came a bit muffled. Then it was clear again, echoing slightly, as if he were flinging it at the mountain.

"It was all evil," said Rigas facing the mountain, "every bit of it, alive and evil. I walked in the woods, and it was like crossing a minefield. The birds were looking for me with their beaks. The trees stretched out their fingers to me. Secret animals waited for me in the cracks of every rock I sat on. Even the owls, they exchanged signals to locate my whereabouts, they had me trapped. There was a rustle in the shrubs, it turned out to be a hare, but that was not the real cause. All of me was vulnerable, I was afraid, afraid in my flesh, and my flesh tingled through and through as if it had been flayed. The first night you came you asked me if I slept out of doors! Even in my hut, door and windows locked, I cringed through sweaty nights and I couldn't make myself small enough, there was always a piece of flesh left to tingle and die of terror. And every morning I began again, I was whole again, I was fresh, new prey. The sky forced me to exist, it made me visible, it offered me up, threw me into the awful arena. Why didn't I leave the hut and go and stay in the village? I thought of it. It wasn't safe enough. It wasn't a refuge. The mountains would still get me; the nights would be the same; big dark awful nights as up here; in the silence houses and people would be abolished by the same devouring darkness. No one could protect me. Every time I came down to the village for tobacco or food, it was as if my enemies up here were simply lending me for a while to the people of the village, and after that I must go back. I told myself that I was afraid of going to live in the village because the authorities might change their minds about me and decide to have me shot after all. They could come and fetch me any day, so I'd better keep to the mountain where I could hide. But it wasn't really that. It was a greater fear that bound me to the mountain."

Stamos crouched on the ground now, and the whispered confession whistled all around him like a discordant wind out of the dark. There were moments when he thought he could see Rigas; he glimpsed a hand waving, two arms raised, a darting body. But the fragments never coalesced, only the voice remained in the end, out of the dark.

"But you mastered your fear," Stamos said in a small voice, still clinging to a credible Rigas. "I heard you out there, shooting and singing. I saw you standing on the rock, there was no fear, you mastered it."

"Out of sheer exhaustion," sighed the voice. "Fear is exhausting, it is a haemorrhage of the spirit. Out of exhaustion one day I stayed up in the mountain, I lived it through. I went beyond panic. It is only a small step. I don't know how long I stayed, as a woman doesn't know how long it took her to have her child. When I opened my eyes again, I was on the other side of fear. There was silence. For the first time there was silence. Nothing moved. There was nothing suspect in this stillness. It couldn't be otherwise; since there was nobody there, since there was nothing. Nothing! I thought I'd go mad with joy. I breathed, I stretched. I couldn't believe it. I lay on the ground. I rubbed my face in the grass, which had once seemed infested with a secret life. I touched the trees, I clung to them. Their trunks were dry and rough, they smelt very clean. I broke off a branch and inside I recognised the dead, passive wood of tables and chairs and beds. I prodded with a stick into the cracks of the rocks; they were all empty. I trampled on the rustling shrubs, and they gave way under my foot, their twigs broke like small fragile bones. And then, I shot down a bird, a black crow, with my gun. It died slowly at my feet, an ordinary death, without much blood."

The voice was quieter. It was punctuated now by Rigas's footsteps, regular footsteps trudging back and forth on the hard ground. The sound was mechanical. Stamos was caught in its rhythm, so that the other rhythm, that of time, habits, acts performed in the ordinary world, was blotted out. And the hut with the lighted door that framed Apergis was like what one sees with second sight, in another country.

The footsteps and the voice were saying: "After that I killed many things. I excavated, I investigated in all sorts of ways. But always the answers I got were ordinary; very poor. After a time, I got no answers at all. For everything was as it should be. The wind made noises, the lack of wind made silence. The dark was the absence of sun. The birds croaked because they were hungry. The sky was vast because it was nothingness. It was very sensible. But I didn't know what to do with it. There was nothing to do with it. I didn't mind too much. I had cleaned up the place of fear, and now it was empty, except for myself. Myself, I thought, now that I am free and the place is empty, I can be myself. I can let the prisoner out of the cage! Bring out the buried treasure!"

There was a pause, then Stamos felt two hands on his shoulders; gently the two hands cupped themselves round his face, directing his gaze straight ahead of him, facing the blinding darkness. "You see?" Rigas said. "It is a mirror. We mirrored each other endlessly. In vain. This place possessed nothing apart from what my fear put into it. I possessed nothing apart from the fear with which this place had filled me. Now there was nothing. I threw out all there was, when I threw out fear, the imagination of fear. My mind was still busy; but busy like a factory worker at the conveyor belt. There were thoughts in my head. But they only turned round and round, fell back on themselves and undid themselves, without conclusion. I had a few memories. But they soon became fixed, as if pinned to a piece of paper; I had to drag them out, and they were always the same, with their stupid, fixed air. Nothing new came out of the darkness; nothing came of its own accord. You have to be reminded in order to remember. A memory is not itself, it is echo, and there has to be another voice to make the echo. I had feelings, emotions, of course. They are always there, they never stop. They came and went, rose and fell, they changed colour and shape without reason. One day I was in a hating mood. The next day I was full of despair. Or of joy. Or cruelty. Or humility. What did they mean? What did they do? They had no consequences. They undid each other, like waves; in the end it all came to the same. Nothing happened. I couldn't make anything happen to me. There was a big hole in me, and everything fell through it. Perhaps all that fear at the beginning, it had just been a presentiment of this final void, a shield against it. No wonder I had clung to it, as one clings to life itself."

Stamos felt the two hands on his temples turn to steel; they slid down to his shoulders, turned him round and shook him. Now he could feel Rigas's breath, and Rigas's head was both a little darker and a little paler than the night.

"When I speak to you," Rigas said, "you answer me; or you close your eyes, or you turn your head away; and then I know I have spoken, I even know what I have spoken. If I hit you, I know something has changed; it is a definite change; you are there to show it to me. You stand before me, extraordinary foreign surface, against which my act collides and is captured, instead of reverberating endlessly in space till it dies away. You hit me back, or you reason with me, ask me a question, and my act is cut loose from me, it is active, it starts living, it makes other things happen. Here I am, stifling in the endless tangle of acts and thoughts that will not leave me—that will not leave me."

The hands dropped from Stamos's shoulders. The pale face, the dark hair shifted, were blurred, melted away. The voice drifted off wearily.

"One turns to God, of course. They say you can find him in the silence, in the darkness. But I had emptied the dark, I had emptied it all. The trees, the rocks had once been symbols of fear; I made them shrink to their own limited shape; they could never serve as symbols again, for anything else. So, without symbols, without signs—no, I knew I could not create him. He was only another thought, as arbitrary as the others. He was only my need in disguise. He tasted of me; when I was looking for something that had nothing to do with me. I knew that wasn't the way. The priests say that God is in you, he is part of you. It isn't true. He is the perfect stranger, he is the other voice. I should not utter his voice for him. I had to be silence, so that there would be a voice that was not mine. I was silence. For days I walked about, absent from myself. It became easy. Silence grew and spread around me. Silence answered silence. My nothingness was offered up and received in full, engulfed into the wider nothingness that surrounded me. They merged like water with water. So perfectly merged that I forgot what I had asked, just as the trees forgot why they were there: we lived on, condemned to eternal absent-mindedness. We forgot why we were nothing. And so he did not come. Nothing happened, nothing changed. Whatever there was in me was as stupid, as useless as the wind, the falling leaves, the night, the tooting owls, the clouds. There were only natural laws. The winter came, the summer came, I grew older. I was hungry, I slept. What was done was undone, and done again endlessly. Hunger, sleep, they were like the seasons; being ill was a kind of storm, cutting my finger, a tree struck by lightning, those were the only signs that we existed, this place and me. That was all the knowledge I could get from nature. It could not confirm sorrow or joy; it could not prove a truth. So sorrow and joy did not exist and truth could be anything."

Now Stamos could see nothing at all. The light from the hut had gone out. The footsteps had ceased. The voice seemed to come from above, monotonous like snow.

"The mirrors were perfectly faithful to each other. They exchanged their nothingness. They were one. The marriage of man and nature was accomplished."

The voice was silent, but Stamos still felt the dark snow falling, falling; it thickened till it muffled the whole world and there was nothing left but to die.

"Rigas," he screamed, "Rigas."

Nothing moved. Rigas was no more a name, it was a word and he couldn't remember what it meant, so he couldn't call it again. After a long time he remembered his hand, his left one, it took form in the dark, because it was being touched. Rigas was at his side, touching his hand.

"So you've seen it," he said to Stamos.

Stamos sighed: "Yes. It was like dying."

They sat on the ground, quite close, like shipwrecks on a raft. Stamos became human again, within strict limits, his body only; at least his body; it was there in the dark; but weighed down by terrible sadness.

"Why didn't you say anything the first time," he complained. "Why did you pretend, coming down from the mountain."

Rigas's voice was down to neutral now, narrow and neutral:

"You offered me a role. I took it. How I took it. I jumped at it. It didn't last long. But nothing so good had come my way for a long time. You gave me something to do. You gave me something to be. What did you expect?"

Stamos shuddered a little; half pride, half horror. He had given birth, unknowingly; it was the first time; and the child was a monster.

Rigas said: "Apergis is offering me a role too. Not like yours! A ridiculous one. He will be at my side constantly, reminding me without pity that I mustn't ask for more. I won't. I am no Philoctetes, I have no god Hercules to tell me why I must serve, or to promise glory after the suffering. I only know I'll take the role. Unconditionally."

After a time, a point of light appeared in the direction of the hut. It began to move in zigzags.

"It must be Apergis, with his torch," said Stamos. "He is looking for us."

They didn't move. The light was coming closer. Apergis found the two men and led them away.

McNally Editions publishes singular, engaging works from off the beaten path. Headquartered at McNally Jackson Books in New York City, our editions are available in the US wherever fine books are sold and by subscription from mcnallyeditions.com.

1. Han Suyin, *Winter Love*
2. Penelope Mortimer, *Daddy's Gone A-Hunting*
3. David Foster Wallace, *Something to Do with Paying Attention*
4. Kay Dick, *They*
5. Margaret Kennedy, *Troy Chimneys*
6. Roy Heath, *The Murderer*
7. Manuel Puig, *Betrayed by Rita Hayworth*
8. Maxine Clair, *Rattlebone*
9. Akhil Sharma, *An Obedient Father*
10. Gavin Lambert, *The Goodby People*
11. Edmund White, *Nocturnes for the King of Naples*
12. Lion Feuchtwanger, *The Oppermanns*
13. Gary Indiana, *Rent Boy*
14. Alston Anderson, *Lover Man*
15. Michael Clune, *White Out*
16. Martha Dickinson Bianchi, *Emily Dickinson Face to Face*
17. Ursula Parrott, *Ex-Wife*
18. Margaret Kennedy, *The Feast*
19. Henry Bean, *The Nenoquich*
20. Mary Gaitskill, *The Devil's Treasure*
21. Elizabeth Mavor, *A Green Equinox*
22. Dinah Brooke, *Lord Jim at Home*
23. Phyllis Paul, *Twice Lost*
24. John Bowen, *The Girls*
25. Henry Van Dyke, *Ladies of the Rachmaninoff Eyes*
26. Duff Cooper, *Operation Heartbreak*
27. Jane Ellen Harrison, *Reminiscences of a Student's Life*
28. Robert Shaplen, *Free Love*
29. Grégoire Bouillier, *The Mystery Guest*

30. Ann Schlee, *Rhine Journey*

31. Caroline Blackwood, *The Stepdaughter*

32. Wilfrid Sheed, *Office Politics*

33. Djuna Barnes, *I Am Alien to Life*

34. Dorothy Parker, *Constant Reader*

35. E. B. White, *New York Sketches*

36. Rebecca West, *Radio Treason*

37. John Broderick, *The Pilgrimage*

38. Brigid Brophy, *The King of a Rainy Country*

39. Ariane Bankes, *The Dazzling Paget Sisters*

40. Vivek Shanbhag, *Sakina's Kiss*

41. John Gregory Dunne, *Vegas*

42. Charles Neider, *The Authentic Death of Hendry Jones*

43. Pamela Hansford Johnson, *The Unspeakable Skipton*

44. Carolivia Herron, *Thereafter Johnnie*

45. Todd Grimson, *Stainless*

46. Dinah Brooke, *Love Life of a Cheltenham Lady*

47. Kay Cicellis, *The Way to Colonos*

48. Francis King, *A Domestic Animal*

49. Felix Platter, *Beloved Son Felix*
